ABOUT THE AUTHOR

Born in London in 1939, M[...] international fame as one o[...] science fiction and fantasy. [...]

He began his career at the [...] edited *Tarzan Adventures* and [...] he later became editor of *New [...] shattering British science fiction [...]en, under his guidance, became a springbo[...] [...]r the finest contemporary talent.

He has published over fifty titles and in 1977 was awarded the Guardian Fiction Prize for the last novel in his Jerry Cornelius Quartet – *The Final Programme*, *A Cure for Cancer*, *The English Assassin* and *The Condition of Muzak*.

Books by Michael Moorcock

Jerry Cornelius
The Final Programme
A Cure for Cancer
The English Assassin
The Condition of Muzak
The Lives and Times of Jerry
  Cornelius
The Adventures of Una Persson
  and Catherine Cornelius in the
  20th Century
The Entropy Tango*

Dancers at the End of Time
An Alien Heat
The Hollow Lands
The End of All Songs
Legends from the End of Time
The Transformation of Mavis
  Ming

Elric
Elric of Melniboné
The Sailor of the Seas of Fate
The Weird of the White Wolf
The Vanishing Tower
The Bane of the Black Sword
Stormbringer
Elric at the End of Time*

Hawkmoon
The Jewel in the Skull
The Mad God's Amulet
The Sword of Dawn
The Runestaff
Count Brass
The Champion of Garathorm
The Quest for Tanelorn

Erekose
The Eternal Champion
Phoenix in Obsidian

Corum
The Knight of the Swords
The Queen of the Swords
The King of the Swords
The Bull and the Spear
The Oak and the Ram
The Sword and the Stallion

Michael Kane
The City of the Beast*
The Lord of the Spiders*
The Masters of the Pit*

Oswald Bastable
The Warlord of the Air
The Land Leviathan
The Steel Tsar

The Fireclown
The Winds of Limbo

Karl Glogauer
Behold the Man
Breakfast in the Ruins

Others
The Blood Red Game
The Black Corridor
The Chinese Agent
The Russian Intelligence*
The Distant Suns †
The Rituals of Infinity
The Shores of Death
Sojan
The Golden Barge*
Gloriana; or The Unfulfilled Queen
The Ice Schooner
The Singing Citadel
The Time Dweller
The Opium General
Moorcock's Book of Martyrs
My Experiences in the
  Third World War
Byzantium Endures
The Laughter of Carthage
The Brothel in Rosenstrasse*
The War Hound and the
  World's Pain*
New Worlds: An Anthology

*New English Library

THE GOLDEN BARGE
A FABLE

Michael Moorcock

Introduced by
M. John Harrison

NEW ENGLISH LIBRARY

First published in Great Britain in 1979 by Savoy Books
Limited in association with New English Library
Published in a hardback edition in 1983 by New English
Library

First NEL Paperback Edition July 1984

NEL Books are published by
New English Library,
Mill Road, Dunton Green,
Sevenoaks, Kent.
Editorial office: 47 Bedford Square, London WC1B 3DP

Printed and bound in Great Britain by
Cox & Wyman Ltd, Reading

British Library C.I.P.

Moorcock, Michael
The golden barge.
I. Title
823′.914[F]   PR6063.059

ISBN 0-450-05721-6

The
GOLDEN BARGE

For Dave Gregory
Pete Williams
and Frank Redpath

This is for old time's sake, with thanks

INTRODUCTION
by
M. John Harrison

THE DEATH OF Jephraim Tallow, which does not take place in this book, is a sordid enough affair, though it might be said to confer rest on what is a singularly damaged and insomniac spirit, one that has informed Michael Moorcock's fiction, from STORMBRINGER to THE CONDITION OF MUZAK, for a number of years. Jephraim Tallow, with his mouthful of crocodile teeth and his brain full of fresh wounds! He is, 'as luck would have it', never at a loss for a word; if frequently at a loss. Outcast, travesty, navel-less and four and a half feet high, fragment or offshoot of the human race, he begins, in a choppy dawn by the eternal river, a quest for the definitive twentieth century stance —— that philosophical vantage point from which the individual, now free to reserve his pain, his compassion and his judgement, can keep watch over the keen inner truths.

Not that he can communicate this. No one else can comprehend his passion (they try to lock him up); no one else can see the mysterious vessel which one morning leads him from his mother's hovel and out on to the muddy water ——

Then the mist eddied. Out of it, purposefully and with dignity, loomed a great golden barge, a barge which glittered with a light of its own. Tallow was astounded ... He was no longer the integrated and impenetrable thing he had been ... He was quite certain that, once he caught up with it, the mystery of his missing navel would be solved.

His miserable, possessive and emotionally destructive old mum, left mouthing behind, is bemused. It is not until much, much later that he meets anyone prepared to acknowledge the fantastic ship of his pursuit. In the meantime his life becomes a bleak and obsessive reconnaissance interrupted by moments of unwanted humanity, as the river leads him progressively deeper into a country bared by war, patched with plague like a dead horse in the street, dispossessed of its temporal frame and yawing nauseously between the first Dark Age and the second, our own. Indeed it isn't so much a place, perhaps, as an era — — whose philosophies are simplistic and deadly, whose freedom fighters are as carnivorous as its faceless oppressors; and it is delineated not so much by landscape descriptions as by grainy photographs of running crowds, by group shots of its inhabitants and their weapons, by an arm flung back as the bullet hits, a mouth gaping open, accusatory eyes. We have seen these bodies, 'hung like dirty washing over a fence' before, in despatches from the Mekong Delta, from Abyssinia and Catalonia — —

The corpse of a dog, swollen like a blown-up bladder, knocked against the side of his boat.

— — —Newsreel footage taken by a man with his head well down as the century fizzes over it like an anti-tank rocket, early satellite communications from the country Moorcock has lately made his own.

Amid all this carnage and despair, armoured by his obsession, Tallow betrays wittingly or unwittingly almost everyone he meets. He abandons children and old men. He throws his girlfriend in the river. Death results directly or

8

indirectly from his every decision. It is not cruelty, nor is it arrogance, for arrogance and cruelty demand one's attention, and Tallow will give his to nothing unless it is the barge —— which coquettes him now, vanishing intermittently —— or himself. '"Every man's destiny,"' he complains, —'"is to become absorbed —— to lose whatever makes him an individual,—' and he is determined not to become human. For all his stubbornness, though, people force themselves on him, and this is the substance of the book.

Miranda lies in wait for him with her green teeth and six-inch heels, a truly Peakean sexpot, Mesmers the philosopher assails his fixed position with the artillery of self-sacrifice; Colonel Zhist the revolutionary, at the last, betrayal staring him in the face, is puzzled and honest: and by degrees Tallow is led into an awareness —— if not an acceptance —— of his human responsibilities. Between them they lever his certainty out of him, leaving a wet socket. His carious sanity crumbles. The barge recedes. Washed up. '"Where does the river lead?"' he asks pathetically (his languor reminding us somewhat of the early Cornelius seeking consolation in some situation of high entropy), and

"It leads to the sea —— and all our souls are only the tiny drops from the sea,"

answers Miranda. It's the wrong question, for it reinforces his suspicion that the sea exists. Tallow: confused by love defused by ideology; his defences have been badly breached; and even when, by atrocity piled on atrocity, he at last succeeds in escaping from his new captivity, he can never really rebuild them. He cannot fully regain his hard original faith. Humanity isn't enough to replace it. He's left only with the hollow pursuit, the final estuary, the edge of the water . . .

We construct our own traps; tumble gleefully into them. Jephraim Tallow's is ideological, or at least idealistic. At the age of seventeen, when all most of us want is a simplified map of the maze with the centre drawn firmly at the centre (when the

9

last thing we want levering out of us is that certainty that it **has** a centre), Moorcock seems to have recognised that obsessive commitment is no substitute for humanity. It has remained a crucial theme, infusing even the twilight of the fantasies with their doomed heroes, their gods and their endless Ragnorakian winters. Now that we are in possession of THE GOLDEN BARGE we discover Jephraim Tallow evolving like an amoeba at the heart of the later work: his first shy public appearance heavily disguised as Elric of Melniboné, who has the **angst** but not perhaps the brains; his brief embodiment as Karl Glogauer, who overdid it a bit, and his inevitable fission into the major characters of the Cornelius legend, among whom the components of his problem (and of his personality, which is really quite complex) are distributed so that they might begin to find resolution in a more immediate context.

This is a tempting line of thought to follow. It can be shown that THE GOLDEN BARGE is ancestral not only to a theme but to characters, events and places which recur throughout the later novels. If, for instance, Tallow has in him a little of Jerry Cornelius (not to mention a lot of Frank), he has also some of Moonglum and Oladahn, and of Jhary-a-Conel that self-appointed 'Official Companion to Heroes', and that Moorcock himself recognises this is evident from the first few pages of his most recent book GLORIANA, in which Tallow, re-emerging as himself after fifteen years or more of captivity in the souls of other characters, is represented as having for a pet 'a little black and white cat'. Similarly, even the least perceptive of readers will find here a man called Slorm-- though he bears no resemblance at all to his namesake in THE STEALER OF SOULS-- and a city called Melibone (sic). But this is a game for academics, and comes down in the end to saying, "Look here! When he wrote THE GOLDEN BARGE, Moorcock was Moorcock!" This is not much of a discovery, and I feel it can be left safely to the many patient critics of the SF Foundation.

Neither is there much to be gained by extending the critical process to the techniques in use here. They are not as sophisticated as the subject matter they handle. The narrative is maintained by the use of the river as a structural metaphor; succeeding episodes being, as it were, floated down it by boat. Much of the imagery in use is a young man's——"her eyes were as green as scum". There is a naked show of influences — when Tallow encounters the dispossessed boy in the ruins of Rimsho, we hear in their brusque blunt exchanges an echo of those which take place between Muzzlehatch and the adolescent Groan in Peake's TITUS ALONE (Peake can be heard too in the names of subsidiary characters).

But this is, after all, a first novel: only those who have neither could deny that as such it should be read for its passion rather than its polish. When it was written, his contemporaries were choosing up sides in the farcical croquet game that has so sapped the energy of the twentieth century, answering 'Right' or 'Left' as their names were called: Moorcock, as we can see, chose to be a human being instead of a Mervyn Jones, a man instead of a Kingsley Amis, and set about forging that amused and compassionate anarchism which is the chassis of the Cornelius tetralogy. The concern which gave birth to Mrs. Cornelius also informs her death; it saw its own birth in THE GOLDEN BARGE. Moorcock's passionate belief is in humanity and in the individual. This book is a plea that both should resist the pressure to become ordinary and institutionalised. It should be read for its Goya-like horrors and its flashes of mercy; and for its final rejection of cynicism——

. . . (Tallow) twists his lips in a smile and his crafty head jerks to one side.

"I know the truth," he says. "I know it. And I don't need the barge. It was not courage I lacked to follow it. Not courage. I needed it no longer. It has taught me what I wanted to know. I have no longings, now——no yearnings. I am free of them at last. Yes, Tallow triumphs, finally. And the barge has served its purpose."

A small, almost imperceptible voice within him keeps saying, **You are wrong.**

11

Author's Introduction

*THIS WAS THE first novel I completed. It was in 1958 when I was very much under the spell of Mervyn Peake and (though to a far less noticeable extent) Bertolt Brecht, who were my great contemporary heroes. It bears almost no resemblance to the novel I had started earlier —— and abandoned —— **The Eternal Champion**, which owed more to earlier enthusiasms, Haggard, Burroughs and Howard. I never submitted the manuscript to a publisher and the book is printed here with only minor revisions of a sort a publisher might make if he had accepted a first novel. Although I was familiar with the sf and fantasy world (I had edited several fanzines and had already been the editor of TARZAN ADVENTURES) I had begun to take an interest in subtler literary forms and I have wondered, while editing this, what might have happened to my work if E.J. Carnell (editor of SCIENCE FANTASY and NEW WORLDS) had not commissioned my first Elric stories and thus started me on a long career of adventure story writing, which produced a score at least of fantastic romances and several science fiction novels. In one sense I regret the time 'lost' in writing books which never, frankly, stretched my talents very far; in another I think I must have benefitted from the apprenticeship in popular story-telling. I gained a number of good habits, and certain disciplines, in the 'sword and sorcery' school, even though the*

13

tales were sometimes lazily or hastily written (though never cynically). And I gained friends such as Leigh Brackett (another influence) and Edmond Hamilton (whose first words on meeting me and shaking hands were: "They used to call me The Planet Smasher, but you went one better — — you destroyed the **universe!"**), both of whom died recently and whom I miss deeply. Leigh in particular had a disciplined narrative style which should act as a model to all those who wish to tell a good fantastic adventure story. And I would not have known, I think, the enthusiasm and kindness of so many readers who still write and who still hope that I will 'relent' and produce further fantastic romances. For the moment, with* **Gloriana,** *I am resolved to write no more of them, feeling that it's high time that I flexed my muscles and looked to new tasks. I love writing, but I could not go on writing in one particular mode for long. Generic writing is too limited. And too often readers and writers confuse genre or substance for form (which is why sf is 'difficult to define' — — it is because there is no such thing as sf, whose best practitioners work in quite different forms — — fable, romance and so on). I think I shall write in a 'heroic' mode rather than in the mode favoured by most modern novelists, the inheritors of the naturalistic writers who (with the exception of Wells and one or two others) have largely been forgotten — — Pett Ridge, Arthur Morrison, Leonard Merrick and others, whose work was pleasingly strong on documentary elements but rather weak on imaginative ones — — but the form is likely to vary. My ambition is to combine the 'epic' story with the 'psychological' novel, as, it seems to me, my favourite Victorian and Edwardian writers could do so successfully (I am thinking of Thackeray, Dickens, Meredith and Conrad). Thus crude allegory must give way to irony.*

"The Golden Barge" is a simple allegory, as were most of my later romances. All my books have a level of allegory (often quite as simple) even if they appear to be more prosaic on the surface. The later ones increasingly substituted irony for allegory. Allegory appears to say one thing on the surface and another thing beneath. Irony allows for more than one interpretation on

the part of the reader. *There can be no 'key'. In one sense the Cornelius books,* **Breakfast in the Ruins, Gloriana,** *are all ironic fables. This book is their precursor, more than it is the precursor of the stories of high romance, witchcraft and chivalry on which my early career was almost wholly based.*

Michael Moorcock
Ladbroke Grove,
May 1978.

Chapter One

RIGHT AT THE TOP OF THE CITY, in the centre, there was a cathedral where blind children wailed among lightless and forgotten galleries. Hopefully at first, in the Manor below, two lovers danced with puppets for partners and eventually became reconciled. In streets, men swaggered from café to café, drinking the while from bottles, pawning their clothes, piece by piece, in the appropriate departments of the wine-shops. When morning came, the children still wailed and the lovers danced, but the men had gone home and Jephraim Tallow awoke, feeling the inside of his mouth with his fingers. There was no blood in his mouth as there had been for months past.

Jephraim Tallow went naked to his mirror and viewed his strange body — stranger now for the absence of a navel. The blood had gone and so had his navel. Tallow deliberated upon this discovery and then, frowning, returned to bed.

A number of hours later, Tallow awoke, put his hand into his mouth and found no blood, slid his large hand down his scrawny length and found no navel. He sighed and arose, donned his sackcloth clothes, opened the door of the hovel and looked out into the dark day full of mist. The mist was coming off the river, close by.

"I must investigate this phenomenon," said Tallow, softly, so that his mother should not wake up. "I have delayed too long. I should have enquired about . . . But now it is too late." He cocked his big head, mused a moment, and closed the door behind him. Shivering slightly, he walked to the quayside, and sat down. Alone, he studied his reflection in the choppy water of a river which was so big that it took a lifetime to traverse. Above Tallow, and beyond him, white and silver clouds lay banked like pillows, softening the day. Tallow stared at the pale sun and his eyes were blank. Tallow was a travesty and an outcast, but, as luck would have it, was never at a loss for a word. Citizens who dwelt in the rotting city behind him were afraid of him.

Now, however, looking at the sun and then the river, dangling his abnormally long legs over the quayside, shifting his narrow buttocks on the cold stone, he began subtly to experience a mood. He narrowed his eyes and stared intently at the ripples of the river as he studied the reflection of Tallow, the man without a navel. Then he began to drag the new emotion from himself, nursing it up to his consciousness until, with an almost physical shock, he was curious. He wondered what lurked beneath the ominous surface of the river now that it was day. Unprecedented, the thought remained in his skull, drifting, seeking anchorage. Water . . . the depths and texture of it . . . had always vaguely disturbed him, but for the first time he wondered about it. It was the shock, of course. It is not every day a man wakes up to discover the loss of a navel.

The mist lay mysterious and chilly over the river; beautiful and peaceful in its calm movement, swirling and changing, metamorphosing into a hundred day-dream shapes. Tallow rose and impatiently strode the quay, peering into the mist. His

18

heart beat rumbustiously against his thin-fleshed chest and he scratched nervously at the insect bites which scarred his tattered body. He looked to his right and his wandering eye was caught by a movement in the mist — a darker shadow which had a peculiar quality of solidity and stolidity. It was coming towards him seeming to move over, rather than through, the water. A ship would have swayed in the unquiet waters, but this shadow did not. It loomed larger out of the mist and Tallow screwed up his eyes, craning his neck the better to see the shape. He remembered a public holiday when he was small and his father, unburied then, promising him the sight of a witch-burning. He remembered the time because it was only that once before he had felt a tremble of anticipation in his dull body. He strained forward, his thin, pink tongue flickering around his long lips.

Then the mist eddied. Out of it, purposefully and with dignity, loomed a great golden barge, a barge which glittered with a light of its own. Tallow was astounded. He looked at the towering shape, agape. His tiny, self-contained world could not survive this second experience. He was no longer the integrated and impenetrable thing he had been, for he had not taken the golden barge into account before. He experienced a surge of new emotions. He became worried that the barge should not escape as it passed. It disappeared into the mist again. Tallow wondered if it might not have been a phantom, a trick of the imagination inspired by the changing mist-shapes. But he reconciled himself. He had no imagination.

He did not know from where the barge might have come. He could not guess its destination. He was quite certain that, once he caught up with it, the mystery of his missing navel would be solved. He scuttled along the quayside, hurrying towards the place where his small sloop was moored. It lay, dirty grey and brown, smelling of tar and fish, low in the greasy water which slapped against the silky stones of the quay. It lay as if expectant.

Tallow's mother appeared from the misty gloom of the alley which ran between warehouses towards the centre of the city. She moved diffidently and licked her mean lips, squinting at Tallow.

"Jephraim?"

"Yes, mother."

Tallow answered absently, purely out of habit, as he struggled to untie the mooring line from the capstan.

"Where are you going?" Her voice was rasping, discordant even when she attempted to speak softly.

"Away, mother." The knots on the line were firm and cemented by grease.

"Where, Jephraim?"

"I do not know."

His mother coughed, like an actress taking her cue. It was a familiar cough which Tallow had never resented, but now he thought it unpleasant, he wanted to escape from it. Her old frail body shook and she looked at him through slitted eyes, hoping for sympathy. He gave her none; he had never given her any for he was incapable of sympathy. Reconciled for the millionth time, his mother clutched his arm and whined: "You won't *go*? Not for ever, I mean? You won't leave me penniless?"

"Of course I shall have to go, mother." Impatiently. "It's the barge. Didn't you see it? My navel might be aboard. Mother, *you no longer exist*."

But his mother had only understood the meaning of Tallow's first sentence. Big tears, disgusting and ludicrous, rolled down her seamed cheeks. She made a gobbling sound with her wet, naked mouth and Tallow decided that she stank of decrepitude "You need me son. What will you do, lacking me to look after you?"

Tallow considered her statement gravely, without resentment. Then after some moments, he realised: "You need *me*, mother — you need me to need you. That is the truth." He shook his head. "In any case, this is ridiculous. How can we

20

exist together now?"

But the old hag had not been listening. She continued to sob, still seeking his non-existent sympathy. "All I've done for you," she moaned, "all I've done."

"You have done all you could, mother. There is nothing left to do."

Tallow completely ignored his mother then. The line needed his full attention. Four feet of wide-mouthed, red-haired, grinning travesty of the human race, he did not squat down beside the capstan to untie the moorings; he folded down, like a spider. His long spindly legs, disproportionate to his body, bent in the middle so that his knees almost reached his ears and his thin fingers deftly began to unravel the knots of the slimy rope. With a jerk and a lurch, the sloop yawed away from the quay and sluggishly righted herself. Nimbly, Tallow leapt onto the dirty planks of the ship and groped for the rudder-bar. He found it and, drifting on the current of the river, moved into midstream. Leaving the rudder for a moment, he released the cords reefing the sail. The square canvas cracked down like a gun-shot and immediately the wind filled it.

Then he was following the barge down-river, the night-breeze in his favour. He heard his old mother's high-pitched voice screaming at him as mist obscured the city and finally the quay. He could not see her. In spite of himself he cried: "Goodbye, mother!" behind him, and then wished that he had remained silent.

"Jephraim! Jephraim!" cawed Mrs. Tallow. "Where are you going?"

Tallow had to admit to himself that he did not know. He might realise his reasons later, but now the only thing to concentrate upon was steering a straight course after the barge.

Lighting his pipe with hands which trembled in time with his heart, he turned up his coat collar against the cold. Turned it up around his ears to muffle any sounds which might distract him.

21

Chapter Two

DAY BROKE.
Tallow had altogether lost sight of the golden barge. Once or twice during the night he had glimpsed it, only to see the mist engulf it once more. With no apparent means of propulsion, it was making stately and silent progress, always just ahead of Tallow's own small ship. Its calm objectivity inspired Tallow; never in his life before had he seen anything like it. The barge seemed to have a singleness of purpose as it ploughed on down the river, never stopping, never changing its speed — yet, always just ahead of him, sometimes lost in the mist, sometimes out of sight around a bend in the river. As he sweated to stay on course, Tallow knew that if he caught up with the barge, even if he followed where it led him, he too would realise what the purpose of his existence was. This was how he felt most of the time. Only occasionally did he find himself faltering, and then he would brush the doubts away. The barge *had* to be what he instinctively knew it to be. There was no turning back now.

But weariness was dragging at his muscles, making his eyes heavy. He would have to rest, soon, and also as he had left his home-city so hurriedly, he would need to take on provisions as soon as he came to a town.

Eventually the sun rose to its zenith, glancing off the water and making it shine like smashed glass, casting on to the river the shadows of the great trees and shrubs lining the bank. Tallow's vision was blinded by brilliant green and black and silver until eventually his eyelids closed; he did not have the energy to lift them again. His head fell against the wooden side of his ship, his legs sprawled amongst the dirty tackle and decaying fish baskets; his right hand was limp over the rudder-bar.

And so the boat drifted on the central tide of the river, drifted past a tall village, two black inns and an iron house; drifted until the sinking sun stained the waters scarlet, and changed the bright colours of the afternoon into more sombre tones which shifted from green into brown, eventually into grey, until all the world was grey and black as dusk came.

Owl-shapes hunted across the darkling, fast-streaming sky and the shrill screams of their prey at last impinged on Tallow's slumbering ears, waking him. He looked around, trying to remember where he was. His back ached and his shoulder throbbed. He painfully drew himself into a sitting position. The contours of the river bank were unfamiliar to him. With a shrug, he waggled the rudder-bar. His ship responded skittishly and this proof of his power over his craft helped him clarify his meandering thoughts. He marvelled at the length of time he had slept and how his ship had stayed more or less on course the whole while. He attempted to forget about his ravenous hunger and kept a sharp eye open for signs of a civilised settlement.

Sharp, vertical silhouettes in the distance soon stood out in contrast to the swaying outlines of the trees. He was approaching a town. Tallow sighed with pleasure and began to steer towards

23

the bank. The trees became more and more sparse, until at last houses appeared among them, some on the very edge of the bank. The houses came closer together, eventually entirely replacing the willows and the poplars until the town was reached. Directly ahead of Tallow loomed a tall curved bridge. His trained eyes easily estimated its height, and he knew with certainty that he could sail under it without having to dismantle his mast. Under the bridge he went, into the deeper darkness for a few moments until he eventually broke out into an area of the river splashed by yellow light from lamps, which lined a small stone jetty. Tallow steered for the jetty, hailing a figure who stood upon it peering through the gloom.

"Hello!" shouted Tallow to the shape. "Is there a berth handy for my sloop?"

"Aye," responded a cautious voice. "Aye — I think so." There was silence as the man began to clamber down the steps which led from the jetty to the water. "Who are you?"

"Jephraim Tallow. I'm a fisher and trader. Or was . . . " He appended his last sentence in an undertone. "Where do I berth?"

"Over there." The dim shape grew a horizontal appendage The man was pointing to an unoccupied stretch of the jetty wall. At intervals, iron rings were set into it. Expertly, Tallow steered his ship until it almost touched the wall, and he reached out to grasp one of the rings. He made his ship fast to two rings and eased himself on to the narrow ledge which led to the steps.

"I'll only be staying until tomorrow morning," Tallow said as he neared the man. "Is this a free harbour?"

"It is."

Tallow could now make out the man. He was young and bearded. His eyes, caught in the glow of one of the lamps, looked wary, and he had put his head to one side as he stared at Tallow strutting towards him. Tallow stared up and back. "How d'you do?" he enquired, letting himself grin in a friendly fashion. He stuck out a bony hand. "Tallow at your service."

"Hello, Mr. Tallow," slurred the bearded one, not taking the hand. "It's a late time to be berthing your sloop, isn't it?"

"It is indeed." Tallow sounded undaunted, but he was secretly annoyed that friendliness did not work on this wary-eyed individual. "I fell asleep, sir."

"Aye? Well I suppose you'll be looking for an inn."

"Very good of you to think of that. Where can you recommend?" The man made no move to return up the jetty steps.

"Cheap?"

"Yes — cheap," assented Tallow, privately cursing the man. He smiled ingratiatingly. "I'll be wanting to provision my ship, also."

"Nowhere open, tonight."

"I didn't expect there would be!" A querulous note crept into Tallow's previously assured voice. What a fool I've found myself, he thought. But he heard the note in his own voice and hastily corrected it. "I'm sorry if I sound a little terse," he smiled, "but I've been on the river for twenty-four hours and I'm weary."

"Follow me," said the bearded one at last, turning and mounting the steps.

Tallow tripped behind him, glaring at his back.

He was led through a series of narrow alleys until eventually he saw ahead of him the lights of an inn. There was no sign over it, but beer advertisements were painted in ornate black lettering upon the windows. Among them was one which said 'Board'.

"This is the place," Tallow's acquaintance said, and he strode on through the night, leaving Tallow no choice but to enter the building from which came the sounds of men drinking, glasses clattering, loud laughter and a babble of speech. He pushed open the door and walked in.

As he stalked up to the bar, men's heads turned to stare at him and quickly there was silence. It was a small inn, shadowy and overhot. A fire moved in the grate to Tallow's left, and

25

three sides of the room were lined with wooden benches. A few chairs and tables were scattered about in the centre of the room, and every inch of seating space was occupied. The men were big-muscled, fleshy fishermen, with coarsened skin and faces flayed red by wind, water and sun. They clutched mugs of beer in their ham-sized hands and regarded Tallow. Most of them had hairy faces, long moustaches stained by beer and tobacco. Tallow continued on towards the bar, self-consciously pretending to ignore the silence and the stares. He approached the mottle-faced publican who was straining to pull a handle, siphoning beer into a pint tankard.

"Good evening," Tallow smiled.

"Good evening, sir," replied the publican, heaving at the handle. "What can I do for you?" He was clean-shaven and his cheeks were brightly mottled.

Tallow's eyes barely came up to the counter. He felt uncomfortable among the beefy beer-swillers. They had resumed talking again, but not so loudly as before, neither were they laughing so heartily. However, encouraged, Tallow said:

"I want a room for the night, if you please, my friend." He cursed himself. His voice had sounded condescending and haughty. Just the kind of voice men like these would resent. But he observed, with relief, that the publican only smiled and nodded his head. One or two of the fishermen laughed, that was all. Sometimes, Tallow reflected thankfully, his size was an asset.

"Ma!" The publican raised his voice to shout behind him. A dowdy woman appeared at the door behind the bar. She was thin and frail but she had large, kindly eyes. Tallow felt relieved, for here was someone he could master. Their eyes met and she smiled at him, like a mother.

"Ma," repeated the publican. "This gentleman requires a room." The woman nodded, walking to the bar, lifted a hinged section and came out to confront Tallow. "This way, sir," she said.

"Much obliged, ma'am." Tallow signed contentedly. He

26

had been out of his element too long. Now he was back again. His step was jaunty as he followed her upstairs.

The room into which he was shown was practical. It had a bed and a washstand, plus a chest of drawers.

Tallow was satisfied. He said: "The name's Jephraim Tallow, I'm on my way downriver. I've stopped off to pick up provisions and rest here for the night."

"Pleased to meet you, Mr. Tallow. We're Mr. and Mrs. Ollert. Have you travelled far?"

"Farther than usual for me, ma'am. I'm not sure what distance, for I fell asleep in my boat. Twenty-four hours' journey, anyway." He hesitated. "I'm following a ship. Perhaps you've seen it pass — or heard about it?"

She folded her arms in front of her and put her shoulders back. "What kind of craft and what was her name?"

"I don't know her name, ma'am." Tallow sat on the bed and began pulling off his boots. "But she was painted — or burnished more likely — golden. No visible power and no sound of engines." He was surprised to note a hardening of her eyes and her mouth setting in a grim line.

"No, Mr. Tallow. We've seen no such ship pass. But if you'll take my advice, I wouldn't be following after her, anyway."

She had not realised that her two statements contradicted. Tallow was astonished. Mrs. Ollert hurried from the room. "My husband will be up in a little while to see if there's anything you need," she said as she left. The door closed with a thud and Tallow was left alone, listening to her footsteps patter away to be lost in the general noise drifting up from the bar-room. Shrugging, he took off his coat, his shirt and trousers, and finally, clothed only in his long underwear, pulled back the sheets and got into bed. There was a lamp above him. He left it on.

Half an hour later he was dozing. The fishermen had departed into the night soon after he had got into bed. He

27

heard the stairs creak and heavy footsteps come towards his room. There was a knock on the door.

"Come in!" called Tallow, more loudly than was necessary. The door opened and Mr. Ollert entered. He stood near the doorway.

"Sorry to disturb you, sir. Will you be wanting breakfast in the morning?"

"Yes please," said Tallow. "I'll be up early, for I want to be off as soon as possible." There was silence. Mr. Ollert remained where he was.

"The wife's said something to me," he continued uncertainly. "About a golden ship you're following."

"That's right," agreed Tallow. "I am." He was completely at a loss to explain the publican's manner.

Ollert took a step towards Tallow. "I shouldn't, Mr. Tallow. I really shouldn't," he said hoarsely. "You ain't the first, you know!"

Tallow sat up in his bed. "What's it to do with you, anyway?" he cried.

"Nothing, sir — nothing." Ollert's own voice had risen, but it was frightened, worried. "But — others have gone after that bloody barge — and none of them have come back! For God's sake, sir — forget about it. It lures men to their deaths."

If it had not been for Ollert's obvious sincerity, Tallow would have laughed aloud. He adjusted his emotions hastily; this melodrama could be relished. "Rubbish, my friend," he grinned. "That ship won't kill me! What's wrong with it anyway?"

"I don't know, Mr. Tallow, I'm sure. But it isn't the first time it's passed here. There was another man who claimed to have seen it — set off after it, he did, fifteen years ago. We never heard of him again — and he was the kind to keep in touch."

"This is ridiculous," laughed Tallow. "There's nothing ominous in a man forgetting to 'keep in touch' as you put it."

28

He reached up to turn out the lamp. "I'm sorry, Mr. Ollert, but you can't convince me that your fear is well-founded. Goodnight." He turned out the lamp, hissing angrily to himself as he brushed the hot glass of the lamp and burned his fingers.

Ollert left in silence.

Tallow found it difficult to understand exactly what Ollert had been getting at. But he wasn't going to allow the man to distract him. He knew the path towards his destiny — if he wished to live, then he must follow the barge.

Chapter Three

TALLOW WAS AWAKENED by a loud thumping on his door. He shook his head, partly to clear it, partly in annoyance. It was morning. The sun shone brightly through the tiny window of the room.

"Who is it?" he mumbled. The thumping continued. "Who is it?" he repeated loudly.

"Mr. Ollert, sir. Time you was up, I believe."

"Thanks, Mr. Ollert," called Tallow. He threw off the clothes and got out of bed. Stumbling over to the wash-stand, he poured water from the jug and splashed it over his head, drying himself on a rough towel which lay beside the basin. Then he dressed. His face was uncomfortably stubbly, but he had no razor so philosophically accepted the fact that he was growing a beard. He didn't like beards, he decided.

Feeling refreshed, he opened his door and walked along the landing until he reached the top of the stairs. He looked down the stairs and made out several figures standing around in the bar. He could only see their legs and torsos. Rather a lot of people about at this hour, he thought. Then he shrugged and went downstairs. Four tall men stood talking to Mr. Ollert who was laying cutlery on three of the tables. Tallow heard Ollert say: "Here he is now, gentlemen," and then there was silence. Four heads swivelled to regard Tallow with eyes which were not unfriendly. Pretending not to notice them, Tallow nodded to Mr. Ollert and sat down at one of the tables.

"Fine morning," he remarked suddenly, startling the four men. They were all dressed identically, in green uniforms, with belts and boots. They had green caps in their hands. They were middle-aged men with bony faces and sunken, weary eyes.

"Yes," said one of them. "Certainly is."

"Yes," repeated his three comrades.

Tallow looked at the door, judging the distance. They were obviously here to see him; but why? As far as he knew, he had broken no laws. Were they policemen?

"These gents would like a word with you, sir," Ollert said thoughtfully.

"Certainly," said Tallow. "What's the trouble?"

"No trouble, exactly, sir," murmured the leader of the men, sitting down opposite Tallow. The way he used the phrase confirmed Tallow's suspicions that the man was an official. "I'm Sergeant Vemmer — People's Protection League. These are constables Bunly, Arpit and Hemmison." The three constables nodded as their names were mentioned. They looked somewhat embarrassed.

"We were wondering, sir, when you've finished your breakfast, whether you'd mind coming along to see Judge Wortmanlow? Mr. Ollert, here, thinks you might like a word with him."

"What's all this about?" Tallow stared, bulging his eyes. "I don't follow you."

"It's about the golden ship, Mr. Tallow." The words came out of Ollert's mouth in a rush; he vomited them at Tallow. "I told these gents. They'll be able to talk to you better than I

31

could. Mr. Tallow — it's for your own good. Just go along with them to see the Judge, sir. Take it calm, sir. They only want to talk."

Tallow was baffled: "What right have you got to tell me what to do? What right have any of you got? I won't go with you!"

"Please sir, please." Ollert was wringing his hands. Tears trickled down his face. "Please, please go with them. We don't want you to suffer!"

"*Suffer!* Suffer — what do you mean? What are you saying?" He stared wildly around him. The constables had softly surrounded him. There were expressions of pity on their grim faces.

"You see!" Ollert sobbed at the Sergeant. "You see — he's not sane. I knew he wasn't."

"It seems you're right, Mr. Ollert," said Sergeant Vemmer calmly. "We'll take him along to see the Judge. He'll straighten him out. It's just a phase. We've had cases . . . like his before."

He put a hand on Tallow's shoulder. Tallow shrugged it off, angry not only at them, but at his own impotence. The policemen towered two feet over his head.

"What are you doing?" he demanded. "What have I done?" He ran, at last, for the door but Constable Arpit stepped forward and pinned his arms to his sides. He struggled hopelessly in the big man's grip. "Stop it! Stop it!" he shrilled. "You're madmen!"

Vemmer smiled pityingly. "That's a joke," he said.

Tallow kicked him in the chest as he was lifted bodily off the ground. Vemmer grunted, continuing to smile.

"That's not really civilised," he said, "but don't worry, you'll soon be better. Judge Wortmanlow will fix you up."

Tears of anger sprang into Tallow's eyes as the constable's grip tightened. "I don't know what you're talking about! Somebody tell me what I've done!"

"It's not what you've done exactly, Mr. Tallow," Vemmer

remarked. "It's what you might do. You might harm yourself. We don't like to let people harm themselves. It's our job to look after them — for their own good, of course." The obvious sincerity of his tone nauseated Tallow. He subsided, allowing himself to be carried bodily from the inn.

It was horribly undignified, and his dignity was important to Tallow, as he was carted like a pig to market, along the winding streets of the town.

Eventually they came to a small grey house which bore the sign: *PROTECTOR OF SANITY — Judge Wortmanlow.*

He was hefted up the steps and pinioned while Vemmer rang the bell. A manservant, in tails and black tie, answered the door. The manservant was tall and angular; he had a head too small for his body. It rested on his long neck like a poppy on its stalk. For a moment, the manservant stared at Tallow pityingly.

"You'll be wanting to see His Worship," whispered the manservant.

"Yes please," assented Vemmer.

The manservant led the party through a hall which gleamed brown, full of polished wood; he knocked diffidently upon a door. A muffled vocal explosion sounded from behind the door. "Sergeant Vemmer and party, Your Worship," called the manservant. "With a Case, sir."

Tallow, throbbing in Constable Arpit's relentless embrace, felt a new surge of resentment. He didn't like being called a 'Case'. But there was nothing he could do. Perhaps the Judge — this Protector of Sanity — would be able to serve his function and protect him from the weird insanity of his captors. Tallow made an effort to control himself. He would have to make a good impression on the Judge.

They entered the Judge's office. Like the hall it was full of polished wood, stained dark brown. A large window, curtained by white netting, let in the morning sunshine. Brass candlesticks and wall-plaques gleamed around the walls. Two comfortable

33

leather armchairs rested each side of a big blackened fire-place. It was a room which had been mellowed by years of use. Behind a large oak desk, placed in one corner of the room, sat the Judge. Behind him were shelves of large, legal books.

The Judge was an old delicate man with pale skin and a forehead which was corrugated into deep furrows. His long white hair hung over his face, his lips were pale and the only relief from the white and pink of his complexion were his eyes which were lost in dark shadow cast by his doming forehead which jutted out over the rest of his thin face like the brim of a hat. His claw-like hands rested on the table, appearing from the sleeves of a blue robe which covered his whole body up to his neck.

"Our Case, Your Worship," said Sergeant Vemmer, removing his cap. The three constables did the same.

The Judge looked at Tallow.

"Do sit down, Mr. — ?"

"Tallow," said Tallow. "Jephraim Tallow."

"Sit down, Mr. Tallow."

Tallow thought the Judge had a voice like soft cheese being grated.

The Judge turned to Vemmer who had taken up a position just behind the chair in which Tallow now seated himself.

"Why has this gentleman been brought here, Sergeant Vemmer?"

"For his own protection, sir." Vemmer coughed. "He says he saw a golden ship, sir. Means to follow it down-river until he finds it, sir."

"I see," said the Judge gravely. "Obviously a genuine Case. Glad you haven't wasted my time, Sergeant. We must save him from himself."

"But you haven't heard *my* story," he cried bewilderedly.

"I've heard so many, my dear sir," replied the Judge kindly. "So many!" He sighed: "Take Mr. Tallow to the Home for Unfortunate Brethren, Sergeant. He should be better soon.

34

Then we can allow him to go on his way — a better, more responsible human being."

"But . . . " gabbled Tallow, "but . . . ?"

"It's for your own good," said the Judge as the policeman escorted Tallow from the room. "It's for your own good, my boy."

Tallow was beginning to think that he was, indeed, mad — so many times had he heard that phrase repeated. Swamped with self-pity, he gave in at last, and, his feet dragging, walked dejectedly down the hall and out into the street where a large green van was waiting. Gold lettering on the side of the van informed him that it was the property of the PROTECTORS OF THE PEOPLE'S SANITY.

Tallow got into the van. It was dark inside, windowless. Ahead of him was a small aperture, through which he could see the driver. The other policemen were shadows around him.

The engine started with a roar and they were off, bumping and jumping to God knew where. Tallow put his aching head in his hands and began to sob. Too late to catch up with the barge, now.

The van sped onwards until eventually he heard its tyres crunch on gravel and he glimpsed a large house and green lawns through the driver's window. Where had they brought him? Obviously, the Home the Judge had mentioned.

The van stopped and one of the policemen opened its door. "Here we are Mr. Tallow, sir," he said.

Tallow got up and walked towards the door, blinking in the sunlight. A huge grey house loomed above him. A stone house; a house with barred windows. A prison.

Surrounding him, the policemen led him up the steps of the house and through an open doorway. Looking back, Tallow saw that a high wall enclosed the grounds of the place. The grounds did not look like prison grounds, they were well-kept and had neat lawns and flower beds. But the strong doors and barred windows belied the lawns. Birds twittered outside.

It was very peaceful. But Tallow knew his duty was to escape and attempt to catch up with the golden barge. He was led to a room where a circular man stood before a squat table.

There were bright pictures on the wall; it was a very cheerful room. The circular man, his body was round and his head was round, smiled cheerfully as Tallow and his escort entered. He had no real features. His tiny eyes and tiny nose were far too small for his balloon head and even his open, toothy mouth was small. He came towards Tallow, his hand outstretched.

"How d'e do, Mr. Tallow," he boomed. "Heard you were coming to join us. We've fixed up a *nice* room for you."

"Thanks," said Tallow.

"We'll soon have you better Mr. Tallow. I'm the Principal of the Home. You're a stranger to these parts, I understand?" He pulled on a bell rope. Somewhere in the bowels of the house there came a distant jangle.

"Yes — and I'd like to know what right you've got to keep me here." Tallow's voice lacked its earlier anger.

A frown crossed the smooth brow of the governor. "It's for your own good, you know, Mr. Tallow," he said.

Tallow felt sick.

A man in yellow overalls entered the room. He looked benign and happy. He smiled shyly at Tallow. A man of some sixty years, he had jet-black hair and a puckered, toothless mouth. He stood erect. Everything about him seemed to be a contradiction.

"This is Mr. Tallow, Harold," the Governor said. "He'll be staying with us for a while. Look after him, will you?"

"Yes sir," Harold smiled. "Would you mind coming this way, Mr. Tallow?"

Tallow shrugged and followed the old man out of the room. The Governor said something, but he didn't hear it. He looked back and saw that the big front door was closed. He was being led down a long scarlet-painted corridor, down some steps. Stout wooden doors were let into the corridor at intervals. Ahead of him a group of yellow-overalled warders were talking. As he passed, Tallow heard one say:

"I had a nightmare last night. I dreamed I went to work without any shoes on."

The others heard this with gravity and smacked their lips sympathetically.

Harold led him to a door which stood open. Beyond the door was a small room, covered in striped wallpaper. Green and purple stripes clashed jarringly with curtains bearing large flower patterns. Tallow entered and heard the door close behind him.

"Make yourself at home, Mr. Tallow," Harold said, his voice creaking. "Breakfast is at seven. I'll wake you then."

Tallow would have said more, but another need arose. He looked under the bed and discovered what he was looking for.

When he had finished he undressed and got into bed. There was nothing else to do. His impotent impatience had waned for the moment. The bed faced the window and, as he lay his head on the soft pillow, a beam of sunshine struck him full in the face. Cursing, he turned over on his stomach and went to sleep.

At seven precisely, Harold shook Tallow awake.

"Up we get, Mr. Tallow, sir." He smiled toothlessly. "Breakfast time, sir."

Tallow swore at him and sat up. It was cold and he was naked. He got out of bed and began to don his clothes which, by this time, were dirty and tattered. Harold tutted and slapped himself on his left wrist with the palm of his right hand.

"Naughty me," he said. "Forgot." He left the room, closing the door behind him. "Get some," he said.

Tallow hadn't wanted clothes, but now that they were coming he decided to wait for them. Soon Harold returned with a pair of white overalls. "Here you are, sir," he said apologetically. "So sorry — very lax — should have remembered."

Tallow put the overalls on. They were too big for him, but by rolling up legs and sleeves, he managed to adjust them to his own size. Harold then lathered Tallow's face and shaved him.

"Now we'll be off for our breakfast," he said. "This way, Mr. Tallow. This way *please,* sir."

With a snort, Tallow followed Harold once more through a maze of scarlet corridors. The place was abustle with the sounds of morning, clanks and cries, scuffling and water running. At last they came to a large bright yellow room wherein were seated, at long tables, about fifty white-overalled men. They were dull-eyed and did not look up as Tallow entered. Harold indicated a place at the end of one of the benches and rushed off, to return with a large bowl of porridge.

"Eat it up, sir," he mumbled. "Eat it up — it'll do you good, Mr. Tallow."

Tallow grunted surlily at the ancient warder, but he was hungry. He stuffed the porridge into his mouth by means of the wooden spoon provided. Harold, taking his place along the wall with some fifty other warders, looked on happily as Tallow ate. In the centre of the hall were Tallow's fellow prisoners. Around the walls stood their warders. The prisoners were eating like animals, snorting. Several were not eating at all but wept into their food. Their particular warders, looking hurt and baffled, shook their heads.

Tallow ate his food and drank the mug of milk which Harold provided for him. He finished just in time, for a whistle blew and all the prisoners rose, pushing the bench back with their legs. Tallow rose also and stood waiting for the next move. The prisoners were a dreadful lot, most of them unshaven, with long uncombed hair; most of them with bent, drooping shoulders.

The prisoners began to shuffle towards a door at the far end of the hall. Tallow followed. He had become used to

38

following other people in the past couple of days.

The door led out into the garden Tallow had seen earlier. The prisoners began to shuffle around it, not looking up, simply staring at the ground. Their warders remained inside. Tallow felt that he was being watched and he looked about him. Behind him, standing on a balcony was the circular Governor. He waved to Tallow cheerfully.

Tallow made an obscene gesture with two fingers and turned his back on the Governor. He tapped on the shoulder of the man immediately in front of him. The man jumped jerkily, leaping off the ground with both feet. He quivered about on his heels and stared with huge round eyes at Tallow. Yet he didn't seem to be looking at Tallow, simply staring in his direction.

"Whaterwant?" asked the prisoner in a lifeless monotone.

"I was wondering, my friend, just why you are here?" enquired Tallow politely. "What did they put you in here for?"

"I don't know," said the man. "I don't know. I don't know."

Tallow persisted. "You must know," he went on. "You must."

"I forget," said the prisoner, petulantly.

"Come now," insisted Tallow. "You must remember. Are you a madman? You look like one."

The prisoner shrieked like a carrion bird. "No! I'm not."

Nonplussed, Tallow was beginning to regret the impulse which had driven him to begin the conversation.

"Then why are you here?" he said as calmly as he could, keeping a distance from the gibbering thing. "Why are you here?"

The man subsided. "Don't know," he said dully. "I liked music, once. They said it wasn't good for me." He cocked his owl eyes at Tallow. "Not good for me," he repeated. "Not good for my *neighbours*."

39

Then, suddenly, as if triggered by this man's confession, the other prisoners wheeled round to face Tallow. They began to chant, one at a time, right down the line. But they weren't looking at Tallow. They were looking at the Governor on the balcony.

"I preferred women to men, but I — considered . . . "

"I invented a gun!"

"I loved!"

"I made my servants dress daily, in pink. In pink."

"I feared my old father!"

"I threw myself into a well!"

The long list continued. Every one of them was guilty. Tallow was equally guilty. Now he knew it. Then there was a silence. They stared up at the Governor. Tallow also turned slowly, to look at him.

The Governor raised his hand. "You were not doing what was good for you!" he said, as if accused himself. "You're all madmen — insane! We're trying to help you!" He frowned to himself, mopping his forehead with a large yellow handkerchief. Then he smiled. "You will all be better soon," he promised.

The prisoners began to march around the grounds once more, eyes on the ground, feet dragging. Tallow shuddered and sat in the shade of the house, trying not to watch them.

In a few minutes another whistle-blast shrilled out and the prisoners began to troop back the way they had come. The Governor was still standing on the balcony, frowning to himself again. Tallow got into line and returned to the hall, thence to his own cell. Harold looked at him disapprovingly and shut the door behind him, sitting beside Tallow on the bed.

"I think you began that, sir," he said, pursing his lips.

"What of it?" said Tallow. "I didn't ask to come here."

He picked up the chamber-pot, shiny and empty, and began to fiddle with it.

"I know you didn't, sir," smiled Harold. "And as you're

new here, we can't blame you, of course. It's for your own good," he said happily. "It's for your own . . . "

Tallow smashed the old man's head with the chamber-pot. Blood and brains erupted outwards and upwards, staining the china. Calmly Tallow knew what he must do. He wrenched off his own overalls and stripped Harold's corpse. Then he put the yellow overalls on. They were not too large.

Then he walked out of the cell, still calm. He strolled slowly up to the front door of the Home and opened it. Two warders passed him, but they didn't stop him. He walked down the drive, smelling the scent of the flowers and new-cut grass, hearing his feet grinding the gravel of the path. A few yards away from him was a large iron gate, beside it a small lodge. An attendant stood outside, smoking a pipe.

Tallow heard himself say. "Got to go into town. Be back in an hour or so." He stared at the lodge-keeper as the man bent to unlock the gates with an enormous key. Then he was walking down the road, seeing the town in the distance and the river glinting beyond it. As soon as he was out of sight he began running, automatically, down the steep road towards the town.

The road was of concrete, neat and clean. On both sides of the road were tidy trees, swaying a little in gentle wind. The sky above was pale blue, speckled by white clouds which drifted aimlessly on the wind.

Tallow thought only of regaining the river. When he reached the outskirts of the town, he took a side-street, then another, still heading for the river. A few people turned to stare at him, but he ignored them, running, running until he came to a road which paralleled the river. On it were several sailing craft, some of them unattended. One, of a similar pattern to his own, lay moored to a timber pole, stuck in the bank. He jumped aboard and tore the mooring rope away from the pole. Then he guided the boat into the centre of the river once more and was away. He had escaped.

41

It was not until ten minutes later that he realised that he had killed a man. As he sped onwards into the late morning sun, he debated whether or not to turn back.

"It's for your own good."

He stared ahead, not trusting his eyes. Then, clearly he saw the barge again. He still had time to catch up with it. He smiled.

"I killed him for his own good," he said.

But even as he laughed, the memory of the blood-spattered chamber-pot came back to him. The crushed eggshell covered in brains and matted black hair. The groan with which the ancient had died, the old frail, naked corpse after he'd stripped it. It was clearer in his memory than when he had first witnessed it. Surely he hadn't really slain Harold?

There was something uncomfortable around the neck of the yellow overalls. He put his finger up to loosen the collar and felt stickiness. He drew his finger away again.

Congealed blood sat accusingly on his index finger. He was suddenly frightened, terror-stricken. He looked back. The city was no longer in sight. He looked ahead — he could no longer see the barge. But it was in front of him, he knew. It had to be — he had seen it and recognised it.

Still, as he sailed on, he saw a battered head and narrow, naked shoulders. Bile rose in his throat even as he steered his boat after the golden barge and truth. The navel! Where was it?

Chapter Four

DAY GAVE WAY TO NIGHT, INEVITABLY, for the fourth time since Tallow had begun his chase. He slept at the rudder trusting to his luck, and the next morning awoke to find himself soaked to the skin, but still on course. The yellow overalls he wore had not been meant for outdoor wear. He had not slept well, for his dreams had been scarlet dreams; but now that it was morning, he could forget. What was one man's life? How did a single murder matter when the golden barge moved surely onwards?

The rain sliced down out of a grey sky, lancing into the waters of the river, spattering over the canvas of the boat. And a wind was beginning to blow. Instead of willows, rhododendrons now lined the banks of the river. They were heavy with the fallen water, sinking beneath its sodden weight. The wind was rising and bending them into rustling nightmare beasts which reached out obscenely to tempt Tallow ashore. He laughed at them, and the wind filled his ship's sail, distending it until the mast creaked.

Suddenly, Tallow realised his danger; realised that he had no cause for laughter, for the wind was driving his vessel towards the luring beast bushes.

Frantically, he attempted to adjust the sail, but the rig was unfamiliar to him and in his panic he succeeded only in tangling it into a mess of knots. The wind blew stronger, bending the mast, swelling the sail like a cannibal's belly.

He tore at the knots until his fingers bled and his nails were broken shreds catching in the tackle. Then, as the wind increased, he had to concentrate on the rudder-bar in order to keep the boat on some kind of course. He saw that he was nearing a bend in the river, and saw two other things; a white flash against the dark-green, and the golden barge just ahead, looming tall. He had been so busy concentrating upon the sail, that he had not sighted his objective. He prayed that he could stay on course long enough to reach the barge and board her — but even as his ship gained furious speed, he came to the bend in the river and his ship lurched and shuddered to a halt — he had run aground on a hidden sand-bar.

Angry and screaming his disappointment to the wind and the rain, Tallow leapt out into the shallow water and attempted to shift the ship off the bar as rain smote him in the face and flayed his skin. His efforts were useless. In a second, the barge had disappeared from his sight and he had sunk to his knees in the water, sobbing in frustration.

The rain began to fall less heavily and the velocity of the wind dropped, but still Tallow remained on his knees, bowed in the swirling, dirty water, his hands above him, gripping the sides of his boat. The rain and wind subsided and eventually the sun dissected the clouds. The sun shone on the boat, on Tallow, on the river, on bushes and trees — and on a white house, five stories high, which gleamed like the newly-washed face of a child.

Tallow lifted red eyes and sighed. He tried once more to

move the boat, but could not. He looked around him. He saw the house. He would need help. With a shrug he splashed, knee-deep through the water, to the bank, climbing up its damp, crumbling, root-riddled earth and cursing his luck.

Tallow, in some ways, was a fatalist. And his fatalism at last came to his rescue as ahead of him he saw a wall; a wall of red-brick, patched with black moss-growths. His mood changed almost instantly and he was once again his old, cold cocky self. For beyond that wall he could make out the head and shoulders of a woman. The barge could wait for a little while.

Chapter Five

S HE WAS A SHARP-JAWED, POUT-LIPPED BEAUTY and her eyes were green as scum. She wore a battered felt hat and stared at Tallow over the short stone wall which reached almost to her shoulder.

"Good God!" she gasped. *"A man!"* She smiled. One of her delightfully even teeth was stained brown. Two others were green, matching her eyes.

Tallow's senses for women had been dull and dormant for years. Women had never been attracted to him, nor he to them. But somehow he knew instinctively that he was going to form an attachment for this one. He savoured the knowledge. For the moment, hugging it to himself.

"Good morning, madam," he said, straddling his legs and making a low, ungainly bow. This was not helped by his sodden condition. "My sloop ran aground and I'm stranded."

"Then you must stay with me," she responded. "That's my house, over there." She stretched a rounded arm and pointed. Her fingers were long and delicate, terminating in purple-painted talons.

"A fine house it is, too, madam, by the looks of it." Tallow swaggered towards the low wall.

"It is fine," she said, "but rather empty. I have only two servants."

"Not enough." Tallow frowned. "Not enough." His luck, he felt, was changing. He would find the barge again, sometime. He could always catch it up.

He vaulted the wall. This was a remarkable feat for one of his stature, and he achieved it with a delicacy and grace normally alien to him. He stood beside her. He looked at her from beneath half-closed lids. "I would be grateful for a bed for the night," he said. "And help in the morning. My ship must be refloated."

"I will arrange it," she promised. She had mobile lips which moved smoothly around the words as she spoke. She was slim-waisted and full-hipped. Her bottom was round and firm beneath a skirt of yellow silk. Her large breasts pushed at the shining silk of a black blouse and the heels of her shoes were six inches long. She turned and headed for the house.

"Follow me," she said.

Tallow followed, marvelling at the way she kept her balance on her high heels. Without them, he thought gleefully, she was only an inch or so taller than he. She led him through the garden of spear-like leaves, finally arriving at a sandy road which wound towards the house.

A two-wheeled carriage stood empty, drawn by a bored donkey. The woman's flesh was soft and itched at Tallow's finger tips as he helped her into the carriage, doing mental somersaults all the while. He grinned to himself as he got in beside her and took the reins.

"Gee up!" he shouted. The donkey sighed and moved forward at a tired walk.

Five minutes later Tallow tugged hard at the donkey's

reins and brought the cart to a crunching halt on the gravel outside the house. A flight of solid stone steps led up to big timber doors which were half-open.

"My home," the woman remarked unnecessarily. Tallow felt a disappointed shock at this inanity; but the feeling soon passed as it was replaced by his glee for his good fortune.

"Your home!" he yelled. "Hurrah!" He didn't bother to mask his emotions any more. He bounced out of the carriage and helped her from it. Her legs were well-shaped and trim. She smiled and laughed and treated him to a gorgeous display of brown, green and white.

They climbed the steps together, leaping up them like ballet dancers, with their feet clattering in time. Her hand slipped into his as they pushed the door open and marched into the hall with rafters lost in gloom. It was a shadowy hall, hushed as a church. Dust flew in a single beam of sunlight which entered by way of the door. The door was apparently warped, for it did not shut properly. Dust swirled into Tallow's nostrils and he sneezed. She laughed delightfully.

"My name's Miranda," she told him. "What's yours?"

"Tallow," he replied, his eyes watering and his nose still itching. "Jephraim Tallow, at your service!"

"At my service!" She clapped her hands and the echoes reverberated around the hall. "At my service!" She clapped and laughed until the hall resounded with the applause and laughter of a vast audience.

A voice like the last trump boomed and crashed into Tallow's startled eardrums. "Do you require me, madam?"

Staring through the gloom, Tallow was surprised to see that the hollow drum-voice emanated from a bent and wizened ancient, clad in faded finery of gold and silver. A livery, tarnished and varnished with years of wear. Miranda answered the man, obviously one of the servants she had mentioned.

"Dinner, Yorchem!" she cried. "Dinner for two!"

"Yes, madam." With a swirl of dust, the bent one vanished

through a barely discernable door.

"One of my servants," whispered Miranda. "The other one's his wife — *damn her*!" She cursed quite viciously — softly and sibilantly, like a snake spitting.

Tallow, knowing nothing of the place, wondered how an old woman could arouse such wrath in Miranda. But a thousand reasons swam into his head and he rejected them all. He was not a man to jump to conclusions. Conclusions were too final — they led to death.

She clutched his hand and led him through the hall to where wide oak stairs twisted upwards. "Come, Jephraim," she murmured, gay once more. "Come my tender Tallow, and let us get you dressed!"

Tallow recovered his self-confidence and rushed like a rabbit up the stairway, his long legs stepping high. They polka'd hand in hand to the third floor of the vast dark house. Their hair, his red, hers black as jet, flew behind them and they laughed all the while, happily, insensitive to everything but themselves.

Up to the third floor they bounded and she led him to a door, one of a number, as solid as its fellows. He was slightly out of breath, for he was not used to climbing so many stairs. As she strained to turn the knob on the door, using both hands, bending her body and screwing up her face until eventually the door creaked open, he began to hiccup.

Meanwhile the wind, which had driven Tallow on to the sand bar, was howling around the golden barge as it pushed calmly onwards; northwards, to whatever victories or dooms awaited it.

"Jephraim," whispered Miranda as he sat back in his chair, sipping brandy from a glass as big as his head.

"Mmmm?" he said, smiling foolishly. The meal had been liberally diluted with night-red wine.

"Jephraim — where are you from?" She leant forward across the small table. She had changed into a dress of dark blue

49

which flowed off her smooth shoulders to cascade like a water-fall down her figure, flaring at the knees. She wore two rings on her left hand — sapphires and emeralds — and around her throat hung a thin chain of gold. Tallow's new emotions were rioting through him — and still a childish awe for his good fortune stuck in part of his mind, even as he stretched out a hand and groped for Miranda's taloned fingers. Pin-pricks of excitement and anticipation were becoming almost too much to bear and his voice throbbed as he spoke, echoing his heartbeats.

"From a town many miles away," he said, and this appeared to satisfy her.

"Where were you going, Jephraim?" This question was asked idly.

"I was — I am — following a golden ship which passed your house just before I ran aground. Didn't you see it?"

She laughed, and her laughter hurt him. "Silly Tallow," she cried. "No such ship passed — I didn't see it and I was in the garden for hours — watching the river. I never miss the ships which sail by."

"You missed this one," he muttered, glaring into his glass.

"Your jokes are hard to understand, Jephraim," she said more softly. "But I'm sure I'll like them — when we know each other better." Her voice dropped lower and lower until it was almost inaudible, but the timbre of it was enough to churn Tallow's thoughts into other channels almost immediately. Some of his self-assurance, so badly shattered recently, returned to him and he disentangled his hand from hers, folded his ten fingers around the brandy glass, lifted it, and poured the entire contents down his throat. He smacked his lips and gasped, then put the glass down with a bang, clattering the dirty cutlery.

He wiped his mouth on the back of his hand, the scarlet sleeve of his new corduroy jacket somewhat impeding his action, and looked around the small candle-lit room. It blurred. Pettishly he shook his head to clear it and, supporting himself with hands planted on the table, stood up.

50

"Miranda," he slurred. "I love you."

"Good," she purred. "That makes it so much easier."

Tallow was too drunk to wonder what it was which would be easier. He ignored the statement and rocked towards her. She stood up, slowly, carefully, and glided towards him. He gathered her in and kissed her throat. As she was standing up, he couldn't quite reach her mouth. Her breasts pushed against his chest and her arms slid up his back, one hand caressing the nape of his neck. The other hand moved startlingly down his back and around his hip.

"Ouch!" he moaned a moment later. "That ring hurts!" She pouted, then smiled, and took her rings off. He wriggled in his tight, black velvet trousers and wished that he were naked.

"Shall we go to bed now?" she suggested at just the right moment.

"Yes," agreed Tallow with certainty. "Yes."

She supported his reeling body as they left the room and made their way up the flight of stairs to her own bedroom.

Chapter Six

A WEEK THROBBED BY. A bedded week, wearing for Tallow, but delightful. Miranda's expert lessons had taught him, among other things, that he was a man. A man, to boot who had learned to please Miranda. The week had taught him something else. He had now a tighter rein on his emotions; could control both appetite and expression to a greater degree.

Tallow lay in bed beside a sleeping Miranda, attempting to shift the sheet which covered her. His eyes were as yet unsatiated by the sight of her lying naked and at his mercy. The truth was (even Tallow had to admit) that for the most part he was at her mercy.

But Miranda was a woman, and took only the right advantage of her superior position. Tallow remained in love with her, and was content. Her yielding and her occasional pleas were so much more worth it when they came. But weariness was fast making a wreck of Tallow the travesty. He slept longer, made love a trifle less violently (though with more skill) than on the first two nights of his stay. Miranda, on the other hand, could never be fully satisfied.

Even now, after ten hours of sleep, Tallow did not feel rested, but nonetheless, he was content. He felt happiness and sometimes sadness when Miranda outraged him, but the joy far outweighed the pain.

He had just laid bare her breasts, when she awoke. She blinked and then opened her eyes as widely as she could, looked at him, looked down and gently, tantalisingly, drew the sheet back towards her chin. Tallow grunted his disappointment, raised himself on one elbow, cushioning his head in his hand, and stared down at her.

"Good morning," he said with mock hardness.

"Morning, Jephraim." She smiled like a schoolgirl, stirring tenderness and desire in him. He flung himself upon her in a flurry of sheeting. She laughed, gasped, was silent for some seconds, and then kissed him.

"God," she said. "You're good."

"Thanks," he smiled maliciously. "That was for last night."

"I earned it, didn't I?" she said, staring into his eyes.

"You did." He rolled over and sat up in bed.

"You need me, don't you?" she said softly, behind him.

"Yes," he said, and then paused, thinking — he had answered the question too quickly. Before he had considered it, he had said, "At least I think so."

Her voice was still soft, unchanged. "What do you mean — you think so?"

"Sorry," he smiled, turning towards her and looking down at her. "Sorry — I don't know what I meant."

She frowned then and shifted in the bed. "I don't either," she said. "I don't know what you mean. What did you mean?"

"I've told you," he said, deciding that he was a fool. "I don't know."

She turned over on her side, towards the wall, away from him. "Either you need me or you don't," she said.

53

"That's not strictly true." Tallow sighed. "I can need you — and I can't. There are things to need at certain times. I need you sometimes." I'm right, he thought — for it was clear to him now and it had never been so before.

She was silent.

"It's true, Miranda." He knew he should stop, but he couldn't. "Surely you see that it's true?"

She was silent.

"Love isn't everything!" he mumbled lamely, feeling uncertain and beaten.

"Isn't it?" Her voice was muffled, but cold.

"No!" he said, angrily, and got up. He pulled on his clothes and walked over to the window, viciously tearing back the curtains. It was raining outside.

He stomped from the room, on his way to the bathroom. He felt troubled and annoyed, but he couldn't analyse the feeling. He knew, somehow, that he was right; knew that he shouldn't have spoken to her as he had, but was glad, somehow, that he had done so. The floor was cold to his bare feet as he walked, and he could hear the rain beating to the ground and onto the roof. It was a drab day and fitting for his mood.

At breakfast she soon got over her former temper and soon, for the moment at least, they had forgotten their conflict.

"What shall we do today?" she said, putting down her coffee cup.

"Ride!" answered Tallow on the spur of the moment. "Ride! That's what we'll do! You have some horses — I've seen them."

"I have — but I didn't know you could ride."

"I can't," he grinned. "I can't, my beauty, but I can learn!"

"Of course you can!" She was now in his mood. "But what shall we do about the rain?"

"To hell with the rain — it can't affect us. Come, love — to horse!" He struck a theatrical pose and galloped from the

54

breakfast-room. Laughing, she ran after him.

They rode all through the day, stopping sometimes to eat and to make love, when the sun shone. They rode, and after two uncertain hours, Tallow soon learned how to sit his mare and to guide her. He was still an amateur, but a fast learner. Since the night he had seen the barge he had been learning many things, quickly. Ideas rushed into his open, greedy mind and he gratefully absorbed them.

So they rode through the rain and the sunshine and they laughed and loved together, forgetful of anything else; Tallow with his tiny frame and long legs, perched high above the ground on a chestnut mare; Miranda, petite and voracious for his attention, sometimes gay, often enigmatic; Miranda the woman.

They rode for hours until at last they came to a stretch of the river upstream, which Tallow had passed a week earlier, but whilst asleep. They came to a hill and, breathless and excited, fell into one another's arms, dovetailed together, and sank onto the damp turf, careless and carefree.

"Your river," whispered Miranda. some time later. "I'll always think of it as yours, now. I used to think it was mine, but I know it isn't."

Tallow was puzzled. He said: "It's everyone's river — that's the beauty of it. Everyone's."

"No," she said. "It's yours — I know."

"It's not just mine, darling," he said tenderly. "Anyone can sail on it, bathe in it, drink from it. That's why it's there."

"Perhaps," she compromised at last. "Perhaps it is, but I know what I shall always think."

"One day I may make you a present of it, sweetheart," he smiled, and he was right, though he didn't know it.

He stared at the river and then, just for a fleeting moment, he saw the golden barge, sailing calmly, as it always did, unruffled. He turned to her, pointing. "There!" he cried excitedly. "There — now you see I wasn't joking! The golden ship! I must have seen a mirage or something the last time — I passed it while I was asleep!" But when he looked again it had gone and Miranda was getting up, walking towards where they had tethered the horses.

"You always spoil things," she said. "You always say something to worry me."

In silence, they rode away from the river. But Tallow was thinking of the barge — and was weighing his thoughts carefully.

Later that night, the rift unhealed, they sat in front of a fire, in the dining room, drinking. She was truculent, unapproachable; he was turbulent, wondering if, after all, the things he wanted were unattainable. So they sat, until there was a disturbance outside and Tallow went to the window to see what was happening. It was dark and he couldn't see much. The night was a confusion of laughter and screams, flickering torches and shifting shadows. Tallow saw that a drunken group was coming towards the house. As he felt then, he welcomed the interruption.

"Visitors," he said.

"I don't want to see them."

"Why not — we could have a party or something."

"Shut up!" she pouted.

He sighed and went downstairs into the dark cold, draughty hall. By the time he reached it, people were thumping on the half-open door.

"Is anyone in?"

"Shelter, we beg thee, shelter!"

Laughter.

"Are you sure this house *belongs* to someone?" A woman's voice, this. Answered by another woman: "Yes dear, I saw a light in an upstairs window."

"Is anyone home?"

"We've got plenty of bottles!"

Laughter again.

Tallow pulled the door back and stood confronting the interlopers. "Good evening," he said, belligerently now.

"Good evening my dear sir, good evening to you!" A

56

grinning corpulence, swathed in extravagant clothing, a cloak, knee-length boots, a top-hat, bearing a silver-worked cane, and bowing theatrically.

"Can I help you?" said Tallow, hoping that he couldn't.

"We're lost." The man was drunk. He swayed towards Tallow and stared at him; his breath stinking of alcohol. "We're lost and have nowhere to go! Can you put us up?"

"This isn't my house," said Tallow stupidly. "I'll see. You'd better come in anyway. How'd you get this far?"

"By boat — boats — lots of boats. Fun. Until we got lost, that is."

"All right." Tallow walked back up the stairs and rejoined Miranda. She was still sulking.

"Who is it?" she said petulantly. "Tell 'em to go away and let's go to bed."

"I agree, dearest." Tallow's mood changed to its former state and his quick tongue babbled, though he didn't mean what he said. "But we can't turn 'em away — they're lost. They can sleep here. Won't bother us, will they?"

"I suppose I'd better see them, Jephraim." She got up, kissed him, and together, warmly, arm in arm, they went downstairs.

The revellers' torches were still burning, lighting up the dusty hall. As the fat leader saw Miranda and Tallow descending the stairs he leered at Miranda.

"The lady of the house!" he bawled to his friends, and they laughed uneasily; he was embarrassing them now. The noise in the dusty cavern of a hall became a zoo-like cacophony.

Miranda said politely, but without feeling: "You may stay the night here, if you wish. We have plenty of beds." She turned to go upstairs.

"Beds!"

The drunken mob took the word up gleefully, chanting it round the hall. "Beds. Beds. Beds." After a short while the word became meaningless and they subsided into high-pitched laughter. Miranda and Tallow stood observing them. "Let's have some light, Jephraim," she said.

Obediently but reluctantly, he went over to the candles and put a taper to them. The hall erupted with light, dazzling the revellers. Again the giggling began. In the centre of the hall was a long table; chairs lined the walls. This was the first time Tallow had seen the room lighted. Grime was everywhere and the paint was peeling. Mildew had formed in patches on the ceiling and walls and the light only served to pick it out. Tallow shrugged and moved to return upstairs again, but Miranda put her hand on his arm. "We'll stay for a short while," she said.

I wish she'd make up her mind, he thought glumly, now regretting the impulse which had driven him to allow the people admission.

They were soft, these people, soft beyond Tallow's experience, pampered darlings to the last; slim, brittle-eyed women and fat blank-eyed men, bewilderedly running over the surface of life, content with their own fear-moulded values, foolish and fooling themselves that they were alive. Tallow could only pity them and hate them. Every second they remained they drove him into himself, retreating into the embracing depth of his own dark soul.

He continued to stare at them from out of his skull; continued to stare as bottles were piled on the table and Miranda was lost among the others, absorbed into their shallowness. Tallow was vaguely terrified then, but his mind refused to control his body and he stood on the stairs watching them, unable to leave or join them.

Clothes were flung in all directions and Tallow saw a blue dress and a black cape flutter outward together. Naked bellies wobbled and naked breasts bounced and white unhealthy flesh was a background for dark hair.

Tallow felt ill. At last his feet dragged him upwards back to the bedroom. His ego had been shattered; but the pain of his loss, of his humiliation, was greater. He lay on the bed, sobbing;

thoughtless and emotionful, his whole world a timeless flood of self-pity.

He lay, his head throbbing and aching, for hours; eventually falling into a fitful slumber which lasted another hour. When eventually he awoke, he was calm. He knew that he had done wrong, had destroyed a part of himself in denying the barge for Miranda's love. He had delayed too long, and the barge should be followed, if there was still time. That was his aim, his goal, his function in life — to follow the barge and to go where it led him, irrespective of what other things distracted him.

He got a large woollen cloak from a cupboard and put it around his shoulders. Then he left, perturbed that he would have to leave through the hall.

When he reached it, he was astounded.

In the centre of the room was a pulsating pyramid of flesh; clean flesh and dirty flesh; soft flesh and rough flesh. It was ludicrous. There were limbs of all descriptions in most peculiar juxtaposition. A pair of pink buttocks seemed to spring an arm; noses lay upon legs, faces on torsos, breasts upon toes.

Such a scene might have disgusted Tallow; instead he was astounded, for the strangest sight of all was the arm which waved at the top of the throbbing human mountain. It clutched a coruscating wine glass.

The fingers were purple-painted talons, Miranda's fingers. Every so often the arm would disappear into the pile and the glass would return, less full, held like a triumphant torch, to its place above the pyramid. Tallow swallowed, his eyes wide. On tip-toe, his bitterness surging inside him once more, he circumnavigated the heap and pulled on the door.

"Goodnight, Miranda," he called as he left.

The wine-glass hand waved. "Good night Jephraim. see you later!" The voice was muffled and slurred, tinged with false gaiety which was not like Miranda at all; normally she was

59

either happy or sad, never false in her feelings.

"No you won't, Miranda," he called as he at last pulled the door open and fled into the rain-sodden night, blindly running down the sandy path, towards the river. Running from something which remained inside him, which he couldn't flee from, which was destroying him and which he was powerless to combat.

So Tallow fled.

Chapter Seven

THE BOAT WAS STILL ON THE SAND BAR, half-full of rainwater. Tallow looked at it dispiritedly. Then, with a shrug, he took off his cloak and lowered his legs into the cold, murky water. He shivered, tensed and forced forward. The boat's timber felt good to his hands as he hoisted himself into it. He stared through the gloom, searching for the bailing pans. At last he found them and began bailing the water out.

When he had finished, he swung over the side again and slowly made his way round the boat, inspecting it as much as he could in the dim moonlight. Then he returned to the stern and put his shoulder to it, heaving. The vessel shifted slightly. He moved round to the port side and began rocking it, shifting some of the compressed sand.

Three hours later, the boat was afloat. Weary with his effort, he sank into it and lay on the wet boards, half-asleep. He eventually arose when he heard someone moving about on the shore. Levering himself upright, he looked over the side and saw Miranda standing there, framed against the moonlight, her hair ruffled by the wind, a man's dark cloak around her.

"Jephraim," she said. "I'm sorry — I don't know how it happened."

Tallow, his heart heavy inside him, his mind dull, said: "That's all right, Miranda. I'm going now anyway."

"Because of — that?" She pointed back to the house.

"No," he said slowly. "At least, not *just* because of that. It helped."

"There's nothing I can say, of course." Her eyes were frank, her body slack.

"No — nothing. It had to come, Miranda. You could have followed the barge with me, once, perhaps, but not now — never. I'd have liked you with me, but you'll always regard the barge as a rival — won't you?"

"No!" she cried. "Oh, no — I'll come with you — *please!*" She moved towards the water. "There's still time — I'll try to see the barge as well. I will."

"No," he said. "It's too late. I'm going alone. I love you, Miranda — but I know my destiny. You've lost your place in it. Perhaps it's my fault — perhaps not. I don't know."

"Take me with you," she repeated humbly. "I'll do whatever you want."

"No," he said, shaking out the sail. "Goodbye!"

But she flung herself into the water and grasped the side of the boat, pulling herself into it with desperate strength.

"Go back, Miranda!" he shouted, seeing his doom in her actions. "Go back — go back! It's finished — you'll destroy me!"

She made her way towards him, flinging her bedraggled body at his feet in horrible humility. "Take me!" she moaned.

The boat was now in midstream, making swiftly away from the sandbank.

"Oh, God, Miranda," he sobbed. "Don't make me — I *must* follow the barge."

"I'll come, Jephraim, darling. I'll come with you."

Tears were streaming down his face, he was breathing quickly, his brain in tumult, a dozen emotions clashing together making him powerless for any action save speech.

"You'll destroy me," he said. "You'll ruin me, my darling; my love." He gave in suddenly, ashamed for her degradation. He sank down beside her, taking her damp, heaving body in his arms and sharing her grief.

And so, locked together in their fear and bewilderment, they slept.

Dawn was vicious; cloudless and bright. Tallow's eyes ached.

Miranda still remained in troubled slumber, but she was on the borderline of wakefulness.

Tallow was lost in introspection, and he could not see a real end to his mental conflict. He loved Miranda, but the barge beckoned. Without her encumbance he might yet find it. He had a responsibility towards her — could he deny that in order to achieve the destiny he felt was his? It was responsibility to himself or to her. There was no way out that he could think of.

He didn't know. The words clamoured endlessly in his head — indecision wracked him and sapped his strength.

He didn't know.

As she sighed and began to struggle towards consciousness, an overpowering feeling of pity for her welled up in him. Then he looked down-river where it stretched straight into the horizon.

Gold glimmered. Tallow acted. It was now or never.

He picked her up in his arms. She smiled in her sleep, loving him. He wrenched her away from him and hurled her outwards — hurled her into the river.

She screamed suddenly, in horror. She knew.

She threshed wildly in the water, calling his name, pleading with him, needing him, terrified of what his actions implied.

"I can't live without you!" The words, a cliché, ancient

even to Tallow, had a meaning he had never realised. They were not empty words — they were desperate words, shouted with truth and honesty.

He sobbed, moaning for her to stop. "It's got to *be*!" he kept saying. "You'll destroy me."

"Love! Jephraim! Oh, God — Jephraim — no, please — please — Jephraim."

Her words were confused, her tone desperate. She loved him.

He clapped his hands to his ears, shutting out her cries. But his agony was still intense.

"My love . . . " he whimpered. "My love . . . "

Soon he could no longer hear her voice. He looked back through eyes which were blurred. He stared at a dot in the water, far behind him. It was her head. He refused to look for long, afraid that he would see the head sink. Then he realised what he had done. But it was far too late. He retired once more within himself.

He sailed on, the barge still ahead of him, still in the distance, until at last his pain had dulled; his eyes fixed on the glittering ship, his mind was blank; he submerged his fear.

Chapter Eight

TALLOW THE DESTROYER, the bungler, the visionary; Tallow the travesty, sailed on, but once again the ship was lost and he could no longer see it.

A week passed and Miranda's misery, his own pain, became an emotion to be destroyed by his mind, once more coldly logical, dispassionate and ruthless. Heedless of his loss, he continued, until at last he came to a vast stone city.

Its featureless multi-storied buildings reared into the grey sky, squeezed together, the narrow gaps between them comprising dark streets shielded eternally from the light. It stained the river bank, a blot on the landscape. But in it were shops which sold the food for which Tallow was desperate. After berthing just beyond the quayside, he walked towards the walled city.

At the main gateway to the city, Tallow paused. A man menaced him with a rifle. Upon the end of the gun was a long, slim bayonet, as grey as the sky. The man was heavy-featured, bumpy-bodied, coarse and uncouth.

"Halt!" he growled. "Who are you?"

"Tallow."

"So?"

"My name is Tallow — I am a traveller, passing through your city. I want supplies and hope to purchase them here."

The man pondered upon this, still with bayonet pointed at Tallow. At last, after looking him over as if the little man were a piece of dubious meat, he stepped reluctantly away from the gate. "Very well," he said. "Go on in. But watch your step, lad — do anything against the law and you'll be hung, drawn and quartered."

Disconcerted and perturbed, Tallow walked into the city. It was quiet, like a mausoleum, hushed and still, as if deserted. But people shuffled through the streets. Mean people, wretched people, half-alive people in shawls and patched rags, grim, unshaven, unwashed, unhappy people who did not even look at Tallow as he passed by them on his way through the town. Eventually he was lost in the maze of streets.

A woman passed. She was thin-faced and had red lips painted on her sunken mouth; her glasses were round and rimless and her hair hung down her face like string. Over her shoulders was draped an old brown coat, beneath that a start-lingly brilliant flowered dress. It was incredibly out of place.

Tallow, attracted by the colour, stopped her. She looked up at him, cringing, her eyes big beneath her glasses.

"Yes?" she whispered.

"Which way to the food shops?" enquired Tallow, not wasting politeness.

She pointed westwards, and shuffled onwards.

Eventually, Tallow reached a market-place, unlike most markets he had known. While it had bustle and noise, the bustle was somehow apathetic, the noise somehow muted — an undertone of whispers and corner-of-the-mouth comments. Only one voice was raised — and that was vibrant with emotion. Tallow heard a few of the words as he inspected fruit on a stall, conscious of the people's stares — corner-of-the-eye stares.

"Sin!" he heard, "God . . . the worlds beyond . . . infinite . . . mercy . . . pity . . . together . . . love . . . " It was a voice with a message and, judging by the crowd around the unseen speaker, people were listening to the message.

Tallow bought fruit, vegetables and salt-meat, then he walked towards the crowd.

A man turned to look at Tallow as the little man stood on tip-toe, attempting to peer over the shoulders of the packed people. The man's eyes were bright, his manner nervous and enthusiastic.

"It's Glory Mesmers," he whispered. "He's preaching again. He's wonderful. But he'll be arrested if he isn't careful — he's been warned not to preach in the market."

"Why?" asked Tallow.

"Because They say he's attempting to undermine Their Authority. He might be too, come to think of it. There don't seem to be any City Guards around at the moment. I hope They don't catch him — or us, listening to him."

"Who're They?" whispered Tallow, puzzled and becoming warier all the time.

"Florum's men." The fellow turned away, looking once more towards the centre of the circle. Tallow gathered that Florum was the ruler of this city.

"My friends, you know me well. I am not a man who hates. I feel only pity for Florum and his corrupt little underlings. I do not ask you to overthrow him or depose his government — all I ask is that you learn to live in harmony together. Forget your fears — your dislikes — and Florum will never be able to harm you!"

All very well, thought Tallow, but what if those Guards do turn up? He swivelled round, staring back into the market place. The preacher's voice certainly was sincere; there was no doubt that he believed what he said and, if the other man had been right, he had courage. The words meant little to Tallow, but

67

he observed that the others were deeply impressed. Then he saw guards spreading out over the market place, coming towards the throng.

"Look out!" he yelled, before he knew it. "Guards!"

Suddenly the rapt audience changed into a hundred frantic, frenzied, jostling fragments, fleeing in all directions. In seconds, only Tallow and the preacher were left — and the Guards. Mesmers, dressed in a simple blue robe, frayed at the edges, stood stock still, staring at them. Tallow acted.

"Come on!" he shouted, leaping forward and grabbing the white-haired man's arm. "Come on — let's get away from here." He hustled the preacher towards one of the many maze-like streets which wound from the market. He had almost to drag the preacher with him. Until, behind him, a gunshot blasted the hushed air; then the preacher began to run faster, but still reluctantly.

They ran on — boots clattering only a short distance away, shrill voices crying for them to halt.

"In here," said Mesmers eventually, indicating a dark doorway. Tallow jumped inside. Mesmers opened the door and they entered a hall which was lightless.

"Thank you." Mesmers' voice came out of the blackness as Tallow leaned against the wall, panting. "You are a stranger here, are you not?"

"I am," agreed Tallow, "Tallow's the name."

"Mesmers — Ophum Mesmers."

"I heard you preaching back there. It — it sounded good." Tallow was lying, he had hardly heard the preacher's words.

"Thank you again," said Mesmers, and Tallow had the idea that the preacher was smiling. He heard Mesmers shuffle about. Eventually a candle was lighted and Tallow was amazed at the squalor of the room — not even in his home city had he seen such poverty and filth. He sat down on an upturned box. "What do we do now?" he enquired.

"Hide for a bit," Mesmers said practically; he looked

68

round at Tallow, who was surprised to see that the teacher was far older than he had thought. He was incredibly ancient. His skin twisted like tree-bark up his face and his eyes were of sparkling blue, a blue which was pale, almost to greyness. They were humorous, wise and humane, zesty eyes which had found life good and worth the living. Glory Mesmers was a human being.

Tallow suddenly realised that he could love this man. He had never met anyone who made such a strange impression on him. He could serve him. There was wisdom in the preacher's old face — but it was not so much the wisdom which attracted Tallow — it was the deep knowledge he appeared to have. A knowledge of a basic thing — a knowledge of the truth — of God? He, thought Tallow, has found his barge. But how? If he stayed with him, he might discover how. It was necessary to remain.

The next few days were perilous days; days which astounded Tallow, for the atmosphere of suspicion and fear which dominated the entire city was like a sickness — a disease which spread, infecting Tallow.

He learned the art of sneaking, of shadow-hugging and of listening. Just as a herbivore's sensitive ears help protect it from the carnivore which hunts it, so were Tallow's ears his protection. Soon he could identify every sound in the stone jungle, for Tallow was a hunted foreigner and the police were after Mesmers, dead or alive.

Being a foreigner, and having physical characteristics both unusual and identifiable, Tallow could not even rely on sympathetic friends, other than Mesmers' small circle of allies. But he was close to the preacher, being his sense of fear, for Mesmers appeared unaware of his danger most of the time; either unaware or else unperturbed; it was hard to tell which.

Mesmers changed his headquarters several times a week, for informers were everywhere. Tallow attempted to convince him that he should leave the town — hide in the hills for a while and let the people come to the preacher. But Mesmers would not agree — he felt his duty, he said, and if he did not share the people's danger then he could not share their fears and hopes either. It was inarguable — but Tallow continued to argue. His respect and admiration for Mesmers had grown into a quiet thing and, for the first time since the sight of the golden barge, had, in effect, opened his eyes to the world around him; he knew peace. Like the city's atmosphere, Mesmers' enthusiasm for life, his faith in humanity, was catching.

It was the words of the preacher which worried Tallow. Words like God, Universal Brotherhood, Eternal Love, Good and Evil. These were all words which meant little to him. So it was not Mesmers' words which inspired him to action which had previously been alien to him. The very thought of risking his life for someone else would have shocked and dismayed him and even now he regretted his sacrifice in one way — though he could not define exactly why.

It was as if he had betrayed himself; betrayed his own character, for, basically, Tallow was still self-sufficient, selfish. He had loved and hated selfishly, with no ulterior motivation. He knew it, and was not ashamed. Why should he be? He had been complete.

But meeting Mesmers had destroyed his completeness, destroyed something of his cockiness. And he still feared the emotions which were growing inside him — even though the emotions were good, worthy. He could not help it — they were not Tallow's emotions, not the emotions of the Tallow that he had been all his life. Not the emotions of the Tallow he wished to be — they were too disturbing and distracting. They had already distracted him away from the barge and now they threatened to drive him to self-destruction. Sometimes he would be unable to sleep, the horror of what was happening to him would be so intense. Yet it took a few minutes in Mesmers' company to make him forget entirely his self-betrayal.

And so another decision loomed, but Tallow dared not admit it.

70

Chapter Nine

THE ROOM WAS HOT, dark and full of the smoke and smell of burning oil-lamps. Some thirty people sat quietly on stools and chairs. At the front of the room, near the door, Glory Mesmers knelt, praying silently, unostentatiously. Eventually he arose and smiled welcome to those gathered in the room. Tallow sat at the other end of the room, idly staring at the dowdy backs and filthy hair of Mesmers' congregation. He was outside, not a part of them, and he resented their presence.

Mesmers' sermons bored Tallow, although it was obvious that the reaction of the audience was exactly the opposite. They would troop in with shifty eyes and bowed shoulders, not looking at one another, but when they left they would be standing straighter, smiling together with bright eyes. This was partly what Tallow resented — he hated this sharing. Although Mesmers' presence did much the same for him, he did not like to share his dark admiration. He was selfish.

Glory Mesmers began to speak slowly.

"How do most of you think of God?" he began. "Is he a formless cloud of all-embracing love? A venerable white-haired ancient in the sky? A fiery sword of justice?"

Murmurs from the congregation. They did not appear to like the question. Tallow received a certain amount of satisfaction from this.

"He's all of those things," said Mesmers, and the crowd relaxed. Tallow sneered to himself. Then Mesmers said: "Shall I tell you how I see God? I see him in you — in myself — in Mr. Tallow over there." Tallow was shocked and embarrassed. "I see him in the walls of the room, in the lamps, in the smoke, in a day, in a cloudless sky, in a cloud, in a dog or a knife. I see him in all of these things because he *is* in all of them. They are him — he is them. God is nothing in particular — and he is everything. That is why our quarrels and our hates are wrong. Our job is to stick together — to love and respect everyone. Then, whatever Florum does to one of you, you will have the strength of all. Florum can fight hate with hate — but he cannot fight love. He cannot fight the strength you will have."

Mesmers continued in this vein for another twenty minutes — answering questions, elaborating upon his theme, calm, friendly, persuasive, respectful of the opinions he heard. And as he talked, the tattered, dowdy people seemed to unite into a whole with Mesmers, becoming one entity, leaving a bored, resentful Tallow on the outside, still.

He waited impatiently for them to leave and then got up and walked over to Mesmers who was obviously deep in thought.

"Mr. Mesmers," he said respectfully; but Mesmers did not appear to hear him. "Mr. Mesmers."

Mesmers remained in his reverie. Tallow stretched out an arm to touch the preacher on the shoulder, but then he changed his mind. He opened the door and looked out into the street. There was a man standing in the opposite doorway, looking at Tallow. He averted his eyes immediately and began to stroll off with studied calmness, down the street. Tallow knew that he was a spy for Florum, he could sense it in every movement of the man. He hastily closed the door, went over to Mesmers and shook him.

"What is is, Tallow?"

"Someone's been watching the house — must have seen the crowd leaving. He saw me. We must leave, quickly."

Mesmers sighed. "Very well — we'll get out by the back way." As he spoke they heard a discreet tap on the outside door. Tallow again guessed that this was no member of Mesmers' congregation — it was an old trick of Florum's Guards. Thumping would alert anyone inside — a discreet tap would mean, they thought, a friend. Tallow knew better. He hurried Mesmers through the house, into the back streets. Soldiers were waiting at both ends of an alley.

His heart was pounding, his mouth dry and twitching. Tallow forced himself to think as panic seized him. He grabbed Mesmers roughly and threw him into a doorway, quickly following him. The door was locked, but rickety. Tallow shoved his puny body against it and it rocked. He kicked at it savagely, frantically, and it burst inwards. Then they were in a small, evil-smelling room occupied by an old man in a disgusting bed. A fire smoked in a grate and the old man looked up, eyes bright with fever. He coughed horribly and saliva dribbled down his chin.

"What's this?" he wheezed. "Robbers? Looters? Is Florum deposed?"

"No — he seeks us — we're wanted men." Tallow could not afford to waste words on this ancient. "Where does that room lead?" He indicated a door.

"Ladder to upstairs — but . . . "

"Thanks," panted Tallow, hustling Mesmers through the door, closing it once they were through. It was not locked. They heard the soldiers enter the room they had just vacated. The old man's voice was high with a note of fear, the soldiers' voices were grunts, impatient and angry.

"I don't know! I don't know! Please — stop it!" Thumps and threats, the old man's voice pleading, the only words they could hear clearly.

Mesmers made to go back into the room. "I can't let him be ill-treated for my sake," he whispered passionately, his eyes full of pain.

"Fool!" growled Tallow, "you're more important than a dying old man. He's served a useful purpose for once — come on!" He grabbed Mesmers by his frayed robe and forced him up a ladder. But Mesmers, when they had reached a loft, still made to go back. Tallow hit him — smashed him on the side of the neck with a balled fist and the old man moaned, then lost consciousness. From somewhere downstairs there came a terrible, animal scream — like a pig in pain, changing suddenly to an atrocious gurgling; a bubbling moan.

Tallow shuddered and humped the old preacher on to his back as footfalls sounded beneath him and a red-smeared bayonet appeared in the loft's entrance. Up another ladder he went, struggling with the sprawling body of the preacher, stopping a moment to haul the ladder after him.

On and on — up and up, through a dark, squalid maze of tiny rooms. Sometimes he disturbed families, women and men, broods of children, huddled like nesting field-mice. He would scatter them in his wild flight, and all he would see would be white, frightened faces, stick-like arms, and shifting sacks which were bodies.

Every so often he would stop to remove a ladder, while the thumping of the soldiers would grow quieter and quieter, farther and farther away until he could no longer hear them. Then he paused for breath, taking the foul air of the building in with great racking sobs, his lungs feeling as if they had been seared by fire, his chest a heavy thing, full of dull, aching pain. His arms were weary from bearing Mesmers' unconscious weight and his legs shook, threatening to collapse and leave him helpless.

74

But he let himself rest for only a couple of minutes before heaving the preacher up and climbing two more ladders. The final ladder took him on to the roof. He hauled the ladder after him, laid it carefully on the filthy stone and swung the cover of the manhole down, battening it with a half-rotten length of timber.

A low parapet surrounded the roof. He staggered over to it and looked down. It was a long drop, some eighty or a hundred feet to the street. Little dots had completely surrounded the building.

Tallow could not afford to waste time thinking too deeply. He had to keep acting. It was the only thing which would save Mesmers and himself. It was four or five feet to the next building. Tallow knew that he would not be able to jump the gap — especially with Mesmers' weight.

Then he remembered the ladder. It was about six feet long. He grasped it and swung it out over the gap. It bounced on the opposite parapet. He tested it as best he could by leaning outwards and pressing his weight on to it with his hands. It felt weak, but there was nothing for it but to risk the crossing.

Once again Mesmers, now beginning to moan, was heaved over his shoulder. Shakily he clambered onto the parapet, not daring to look down. Then he placed a foot on the ladder and ran across it. He had absolutely no recollection of the crossing. Only the first few steps outwards, then he was safe and hauling the ladder after him.

Four times he made crossings from building to building, with gaining confidence, but with no memory of the drop beneath him. Then, feeling sick and weary, he collapsed onto the greasy stone of a roof. His head was near Mesmers' head and the old man was groaning, his eyes flickering open, his old, delicate hands fluttering like white doves up to his head where Tallow had hit him.

Tallow looked at him. "We're saved," he whispered. "I saved you."

75

Mesmers' tone was chiding, almost angry. He said: "At what expense, Tallow?" That was all. Then he was silent again. They remained like this for several hours until darkness came and they slept.

Tallow awoke just as the night was changing into the grey of morning. He stretched aching limbs and yawned. The cold morning air bit into his throat and lungs, reviving him. Mesmers was gone.

It took several seconds for Tallow to realise this. He was up in an instant, then, looking around the expanse of grey roof. Mesmers was not there, and the ladder remained where Tallow had dropped it the previous night.

But a manhole into the roof was open, like a fledgeling's mouth, agape in surprise, mimicking Tallow's own expression.

He went over to the hole and stared downwards. He could see nothing but blackness. Desperately he wriggled into the hole, hung by his hands and dropped, landing on bare boards. There was no one in the room. He hastily made for the door and tore it open. No one. This house was better designed than the one through which he had made his escape. A landing was outside and stairs led downwards. He ran for the stairs, leaping down them, heedless of the noise he was making. No one came out of doors to stare at him. The house might have been empty for all the notice that was taken of Tallow as he leaped desperately downwards.

He saw Mesmers' robe, now streaked with filth, disappearing out of the street door as he reached the last landing. Not daring to call, he ran after him, eventually catching him up as he turned a corner of the street.

"Why did you leave me, Mr. Mesmers?" he gasped.

"I do not want you to sin for me again, Tallow," replied the preacher without looking at the little man or slackening his pace.

"But you need me, sir — you need me. You'd be in Florum's prison if it wasn't for me."

76

"I do not need, you, Tallow — you have only succeeded in interfering."

Tallow's mind was a whirlpool of desperate thoughts as he tried to understand the import of Mesmers' words.

"Then I need you," he said craftily, and truthfully. "I need you, sir. Don't leave me like this after all I've done to help you. Help me now, sir. Help me."

"You have rejected the kind of help I can give you; you may stay with me, however, on condition that you listen to what I have to say. Stop interfering in my destiny."

"But your destiny is mine."

"It might have been," said Mesmers, regret in his voice. "It might well have been — once."

"What have I done wrong — tell me and I'll make amends. I swear it."

Mesmers stopped at a door. Tallow knew it was one of their places of refuge. He turned and contemplated Tallow, pity in his wise eyes.

"Your reasons for helping me have not been the right reasons. I have been responsible for the death of a man — because of you. I do not *need* you Tallow — our association will lead to further violence. More death — more unhappiness for these unhappy people. I offer them life — you could bring them nothing but pain and grief — your own pain, your own grief. Can't you see that?"

"No! You are unjust."

"I have tried to be just — perhaps you are right. But I think not. Your sins are grey about you."

"What sins? I have never sinned — I would know it if I had. I do not know it."

Mesmers sighed and entered the house. Tallow followed him, clutching at his robe. "I do not know it," he repeated, "so I have not sinned — have I? If what you said about every man knowing deep in himself that he has sinned is true — then I am innocent." Tallow felt a tiny surge of triumph.

77

Mesmers closed the door and looked deeply into Tallow's eyes, the pity still in his gaze — a hopeless pity.

"If you do not know, then perhaps my faith is wrong — I hope not. But if you do not know — then all I have said is doubly true."

Suddenly Tallow felt relieved and his attitude altered. His affection for Mesmers, this alien self-sacrifice, had been like chains on his legs for too long. Now he saw a way out of his dilemma. This was the turning point; he could be free again.

"Fool!" he sneered. "Blind idiot! You are no visionary! You are nothing in this city, you waste your time upon others and they hate you for it. *You* are the person who matters — not the others, they are dragging you down with them — and I would have followed you. I have realised this at last, thank God."

Mesmers stood in silence, his ancient face calm. Tallow raved on, submerging the feeling of insignificance which Mesmers' stare instilled in him; submerging the feelings in rage: "You've denied your own destiny. I'll leave you — though I tried to save you. I have a purpose greater than yours!"

He wrenched the door open and went out into the street.

"Come back, Jephraim!" said Mesmers suddenly. "You'll be caught and shot if you go out at this hour! Come back man. If you must go, wait until nightfall!"

But Tallow was heedless of the preacher's warning. He marched out towards the river, knowing that the barge would take weeks to catch up with. But it was his only hope.

Mesmers called again, urgently. Tallow ignored the cry. His destiny beckoned.

Chapter Ten

S OON, TALLOW'S CALCULATING MIND came once more to his aid as he realised his danger. He kept to back streets, following tortuous alleys to the river-side, uncertain of how he was going to get out of the city, for every gate was guarded.

He slunk onwards, his rage quiet and unreasonable within him. He was determined to get to the gates and then decide what to do when faced with the decision.

It took him two hours of pausing, hiding and scurrying before he could reach the city wall. Following it along, he finally came to a gate. Three Guards leant against the wall, wary and watchful. They had increased the number of soldiers — probably because of the chase of the previous day.

He shrunk back onto shadow as one of them turned to look in his direction. But he had not been quick enough.

"Hey! You! Come out of that alley and show yourself." Tallow swallowed down the panic which rose inside him and ran hastily back the way he had come.

"I could swear it was the red-haired midget we're after!" he heard the Guard shout to his friends. "Cript, come with me — there's a reward on his head!"

Now Tallow's only emotion was fear; it embraced him — dominated him — drove him recklessly away from the shouting Guards. He fled.

He fled for three days — ruthlessly hunted. He became a frightened animal, cowering and afraid; skulking in sewers, hiding in the houses of a few people he thought he could trust. But betrayal always sent him running again. Three days were spent in scuttling and skulking; they were weary days, for he dare not allow himself to succumb to sleep. Cocky, self-reliant, selfish Tallow learned what it was to depend on others — to trust a glib-tongued informer and discover that the man was leading soldiers to his hiding place. Soon Tallow forgot everything save his need to escape.

Then, one day, Mesmers found him.

"You are sick," said Mesmers to the unshaven, shivering wretch who pleaded to him. "You should have listened, my friend."

"I'll listen now — I will. Save me — hide me — that's all I ask, sir. Save me — I should have listened. I've been pursued and shot at — I've been fooled and betrayed. You were right, Mr. Mesmers — oh, you were right, sir. Hide me now — please."

Mesmers frowned, hating what Tallow had become, hating what had made him the thing he now was. "I will hide you until it is safe for you to leave," he said. "Then you will go away from here."

"But suppose they catch me when I leave — they'll kill me. My blood'll pour out — I'll die. They'll torture me, sir, for you. They'll want to know where you are and they'll make me tell them. They will, sir — they will. Save me." Tallow sobbed horribly, clawing at Mesmers' robe with a hand caked in filth.

"We'll see," said Mesmers. "But first you must rest." Several young men, followers of the preacher, came forward at a signal and grasped Tallow, dragging him away from the old man.

"Put him to bed, my friends," murmured Mesmers, looking at Tallow. "Make him sleep. Later we'll attempt to smuggle him out. I owe him that."

But it was not easy for Tallow to sleep. Mesmers or one of his followers remained always at Tallow's bedside, listening to the moans and screams as Tallow relived the three days of terror in his nightmares. Occasionally Tallow would wake up, shrieking and roaring and he had to be quietened. Silence was the order of the day of Florum's rule.

It was Mesmers with his quiet voice and persuasive manner who virtually hypnotised Tallow into a deep sleep; Mesmers who effected Tallow's cure and helped the little man recover some of his self-respect and assurance. Mesmers' against his better judgement, built a new Tallow after the pattern of the old — for he could not build an entirely new Tallow without new materials. He gave Tallow back his cockiness. He gave Tallow what had been taken away from him. And he knew that his gift was a seed — a seed which had nearly destroyed the man he was now saving. If Mesmers had not been an optimist, he would have despaired.

Soon, Tallow was grinning his old fool's grin, his wide-mouthed, sharp-toothed grin — his crocodile smile. He sat up in the bed — Mesmers' bed — and cocked his head at the preacher.

"Thank you," he said, without gratitude. "You certainly knew how to cure me, didn't you? The credit's square now. I saved you; you saved me. I'll be on my way as soon as I've rested a little more."

Mesmers nodded sadly and got up. There were dark patches under his eyes which showed that he had slept even less than usual. He walked tiredly away from Tallow, and his shoulders drooped. "I'll make sure you leave the town safely," he sighed, "but I shan't see you again, Mr. Tallow."

"Goodbye," grinned Tallow, folding his arms behind his

head and sinking back onto his pillows. "I hope you make out!"

"Goodbye." Mesmers left slowly and was soon gone. Tallow heard the outer door close.

Two days later an old woman in a shawl shuffled away from the house where Tallow had been resting. The old woman was Tallow.

In his disguise, Tallow hoped to reach the quayside and mingle with the crowd which gathered there every day to watch the ships come in. There, Mesmers' followers had said, he might be able to stow away on one of the foreign boats — or steal a boat if he could do so without too much risk.

The disguise was perfect. He acted his part perfectly, a battered basket on one arm, the other hand clutching his shawl about his head, hiding his face in shadow.

No one even glanced at him — there were so many poor old women in the city. When he reached the main street which led towards the quayside, he joined a slowly-moving crowd which was walking purposefully in the direction of the river. There was a fence cutting off the dock area from the rest of the city and the fence was guarded, but the crowd was allowed through. His heart thumping, Tallow passed a Guard he recognised, but the Guard was staring hard at a young girl, to his left, who walked behind her father. The Guard leered, all his thoughts concentrated, for the moment, on the girl. Tallow began to view things with more calm. So far, it had been easier to get to the quay than he had originally thought.

The tall ships came into sight and Tallow was instantly filled with longing. Each ship offered escape — and more. Each ship was a means of following the golden barge. Several small one-man boats of a type Tallow was familiar with, bobbed among the larger craft. One of those would be excellent.

He followed the crowd, coming to a standstill on one side of the quay. Men were busy loading and unloading goods to and from the many ships. But the place was still thick with sour-faced Guards, watchful Guards, distrustful of any sign which

82

was other than normal.

Tallow relaxed and waited for his opportunity.

It came at last when there was a disturbance on the opposite side of the quay. Tallow could not make out what was causing it, but it held the Guards' attention. They swung menacing rifles towards it and Tallow heard rough voices demanding something. The Guards began to move in the direction of the noise. Tallow started running.

He ran for the river, hearing a yell behind him. A rifle-shot exploded quite close to him, but he kept running. Then Guards were converging from all directions, some lumbering to cut off his escape towards the water. He stared around him wildly, encircled by gleaming bayonets.

Then, desperately, he pointed towards the crowd — "He's in there — Mesmers is in the crowd. He made me run out so that he could get away." The Guards wavered, uncertain.

"It's true!" shouted Tallow. "He'll get away. He's wanted dead or alive!"

Guns began to level on the crowd. Seeing their danger, the people attempted to draw back. A captain bawled an order: "Stay where you are — nobody move."

But the crowd was frightened now. They began to run, knocking one another aside in their haste.

"Fire! Fire!"

Gunshots cracked and two men fell.

"Stop!"

But the gunshots had served to turn the crowd into a panicking mass. They scattered in all directions over the quayside. The Guards fired blindly into them, attempting to stop the rush for the fence. The girl who had distracted the gate Guard's attention fell, screaming. Two boys leapt high and fell, kicking, to the ground, clutching their thighs, trying to stop the pain which flowed in their bodies.

Tallow ripped off his shawl, and turned towards the river. He dived in and struck out for a motor-boat moored nearby.

Two of the Guards saw him. They aimed their guns at him. Bullets splattered around him in the water, but he reached the boat.

He hauled himself into the tiny cabin and started the motor. It roared. Zestfully the propeller churned the muddy waters of the river, driving the boat forward.

Tallow laughed at the helpless Guards and ducked as a bullet whistled by. Several soldiers ran for two larger boats moored together. Tallow increased speed and had soon left the quayside, laughing all the while in mad relief.

On the quayside, the people were still running — running towards the opposite end, where the original disturbance had came from. As if participating in a macabre game of hare-and-hounds, they left a trail of bleeding bodies in their wake. A smaller group, who had remained still, staring at Tallow, while the larger crowd had fled, made no move to run. The crowd reached them and engulfed them.

Two of the members of the group fell dead as bullets tore into the mass of flesh which screamed in panic. Some of them were climbing the fence now, many to be picked off by bullets. Bodies hung like dirty washing over the fence. Then the crowd stopped and looked fearfully back at the soldiers.

The captain shouted again: "Stop, now! We wish to make an inspection. You have nothing to fear if you are innocent!" Cowed, the crowd subsided.

The captain and two lieutenants moved among the people, inspecting the bodies and the faces of the living.

One of the soldiers called to the captain.

"He was right, sir — look!"

He pulled a dark cloak away from an ancient, blue-robed man. A man with white hair and staring, humane eyes. A man with a pale face, with skin of twisted tree-bark, down which blood now coursed — a hundred miniature rivers of red, from head, from mouth and from two wounds in the body.

"It's Mesmers all right, sir. I've seen him several times,

preaching in the market place. We've got him at last, sir."

"Yes," smiled the captain, like a shark. "It's him. So our little friend didn't lie. Is the preacher still alive?"

"Yes, sir. I think so." The lieutenant bent down beside the old man. His eyes flickered.

"I — was — wrong — I suppose," gasped Mesmers. "I should not — have - rebuilt — him. He — destroyed — me — as I — knew he would."

"What's he talking about?"

"Don't know — probably about his little rat of a friend, sir. These people are all the same — betray anyone if they think they're saving themselves. Shouldn't be surprised if the little man was the red-haired midget who rescued Mesmers a few times in the last couple of weeks. Funny thing, that — saving him, then getting him killed."

He stared down at Mesmers. The preacher stared back, glassily, soullessly. Mesmers was dead.

"What a bastard thing to do," murmured the lieutenant, staring down-driver. Tallow's boat had disappeared, but the two larger craft were giving chase, overweighted with men. "What a bastard thing to do!"

"Come on, lieutenant," said the captain impatiently, "let's get the corpse to headquarters. There should be a nice little bit in this for all of us — you'll be able to buy your girlfriend that ring she wants, now."

The young soldier smiled, cheering up at once: "So I shall, sir," he said. "Hadn't thought of it."

Two Guards hefted Mesmers' pitiful corpse between them and began to cart it off. The young lieutenant looked back once more down-river. "Funny, that . . . " he said to himself, following his captain.

Meanwhile, a jaunty Tallow, unaware of the death of Mesmers, easily outdistanced the overloaded pursuing boats and looked happily ahead, hoping for a glimpse of the barge.

Chapter Eleven

MIRANDA DIDN'T LIKE THE LOOK OF THE CAPTAIN, but she had no choice, his was the only ship available. She put her bag down at her feet and looked up at him. His eyes moved over her body, not meeting her eyes for some seconds. She pursed her lips.

"How far are you going down-river?" she asked.

"How far?" He rubbed his stubbly chin with one hand and scratched the back of his inhabited head with the other.

"How far are you going?"

"Two hundred miles, maybe, more or less."

"Fair enough. Will this pay for it?" She displayed a bag of coin. "It's gold."

"Yes," he said. She could tell by his eyes that it was more than enough.

"Of course I'll want a private cabin," she added quickly.

"Of course," he said tonelessly.

"Then I'll get on board," she said in a hard voice, quite

unlike her usual one. "When do you cast off?"

"Four o'clock," he replied. "In an hour's time."

"Thanks," she said.

She had left her arrangements for as late as possible. The man she had obtained the money from might follow her and demand that she return. Not that she had been particularly unhappy with him; it was simply that he wasn't Tallow. Her search for, and pursuit of Tallow had become an obsession. She still loved him.

The cabin was bare of ornament, but clean, though small. A bunk was erected on the port side and a locker opposite it. That was all. The sailor who showed her the cabin said; "I'll bring you hot water for washing every morning at eight, ma'am. You'll get your breakfast in your cabin at about eight-thirty, give or take a bit."

"Thank you." She smiled. The sailor was big and handsome. He looked at her shyly — the way she liked some men to look at her. "The trip should be pleasant."

"I hope so, ma'am," he said.

"So do I." She smiled again, looking at him through hinting eyes. She couldn't help it — it was habit with her. Anyway, she qualified, my love for Tallow isn't purely sexual, otherwise I wouldn't bother to do what I'm doing now. I'll follow him — but I certainly shan't bother to be faithful to the bastard. Her deep, aching longing for her deserter was eased a little by his thought. She smiled a third time: to herself.

Hers had been a long, hard journey. When she had eventually struggled ashore, she had had to walk miles to a town. There she had easily made friends, eventually winding up with the mayor. From him she had procured her fare down as far as the next town — for she had to leave quite suddenly when the mayoress discovered her husband's attachment.

And so she had gone on, getting her fare, moving when she could — or when she had to. And at last she had found a rich man and a ship travelling an appreciable distance. The two

87

combined had been an excellent stroke of luck.

She still didn't know why she was following Tallow. He had treated her atrociously; but she knew he still loved her. Her ego had been shattered, that was all — and she was not altogether happy about her soaking and subsequent travelling. One part of her mind maliciously promised her that she would make Tallow cringe when she caught up with him. And she was going to catch up with him — it was necessary.

So she began to unpack her few belongings, waiting impatiently for the ship to leave the berth. If she knew her Tallow, he would not have got very far ahead.

Chapter Twelve

TALLOW HAD CAUGHT UP WITH THE BARGE. It was only about quarter of a mile distant. But the weather was bad. Wind howled around him and the river was choppy and dangerous at this wide stretch. The swirling water and wind did not affect the barge in the slightest. It went purposefully on — calm, implacable, imperturbable, moving down the river as if the water did not exist. The currents which so confused Tallow had absolutely no effect upon the steadily-moving golden ship. They did not shift it one inch from the path it steered in the very middle of the river. Tallow was not amazed or confused by this. He had come to expect it. Otherwise there would have been no point in following. He was excited, however, and annoyed at the sudden change in the weather, which had occurred just as he had sighted the barge again. It was always the same. Whenever he had a chance to catch up with it, something happened to divert him — man or nature. Was it his doom to follow it eternally — or was there a chance of it leading him to something? At that moment, for some reason, as he battled with the elements, it did not seem to matter at all.

A few days earlier, when he had left the city in such haste, he had been hard-pressed to elude the gunboats and river-bank patrols which searched for him, but now Florum's men had given up the chase.

Tallow regretted the fact that he had been responsible for a number of the citizens losing their lives, but he balanced this by telling himself that if he had been caught and tortured, he might have betrayed Mesmers and he still felt admiration for the preacher whilst abhoring his ideals.

What a companion on a voyage such as mine, he thought. This is his place, beside me, following the barge. But he had a nagging feeling in the back of his mind that perhaps Mesmers had already followed the barge — and discovered its ultimate destination. Hadn't the old preacher said something to that effect at some time? He thought so. But he couldn't remember the moment. Perhaps when he had been raving after his ordeal? No — it wasn't any good, he couldn't be certain.

But suppose the barge led him to those horrible acts of self-sacrifice of which Mesmers had been guilty? No — he had to be sure that the barge led a man to his personal destiny — depending on the man. If he, Tallow, was strong, as he was, then his destiny would be that much more certain, surely?

Tallow saw that his boat was being forced to one side of the river bank. Hastily, he corrected the course and plugged on after the barge which was swiftly outdistancing him.

He cursed and fumed, but it was no good; the barge, without increasing its speed, was making far better progress than he was.

Eventually it had disappeared from his sight once more and, for the moment, he gave up the chase. There would be only one thing to do — wait for better weather, and then attempt to make up for lost time.

He guided the boat over to the river bank and tied it up

to a tree-trunk. The boat had been well-stocked with equipment and provisions, including a tent. He would pitch the tent on the shore and sleep, then he would continue in the morning.

Making sure that the boat was moored securely, he jumped onto the bank, throwing his tent in front of him. The ground was damp and squelched beneath his feet as he walked through the silent wood, water dripping from the branches, mingling with the rain and sweat on his face. It was peaceful in the woods, in contrast to the turbulent waters of the river. A good place to rest.

In a glade, shielded by trees, the ground had absorbed much of the water into itself — and the surface, protected by turf, made a better spot than most for pitching his tent. As he began to adjust the tent-poles and check the guy-ropes, he heard a peculiar wailing noise coming from a hillock a few yards away.

Curious, he went over to investigate and found a baby.

It was an ugly, skinny child, about two months old. It lay in a cot of woven twigs and sodden blankets covered it. Tallow bent down and removed the blankets, picked up the child and replaced the damp cloth with his cloak turned inside out. The baby ceased to wail and began to gurgle happily.

Tallow picked up the cot and took it over to where he had planned to pitch the tent. Leaving the child, he erected the tent and placed the cot inside.

He decided that the baby had probably been left out to starve by some woman who couldn't keep it. Well, it could wait until morning. He managed to feed it some milk and then got into his sleeping bag and slept, heedless, during the night, of the occasional wails from the baby.

Next morning he set off in the opposite direction from the river, intent on discovering the baby's owner. He reasoned that there must be some collection of cottages, or town, nearby.

He was right. Coming out of the wood on a morning which was sunny, bright and cloudless, he saw the smoke of chimneys some distance away to the west. The baby's cot was heavy in his arms, but he didn't want to be responsible for its death and knew from experience that people were usually soft enough to take a baby in. All he knew was that he wasn't.

As he got nearer to the village, he noticed that the fields surrounding it were barren. Trees were rotting and an evil smell pervaded the whole area. Occasionally he passed a dead animal, its stomach bloated and distended, flies crawling over it. Cattle, horses, sheep and pigs were scattered like seeds over the country-side. A few wild deer, rabbits and hares were also in presence, in the same condition as the domestic animals. It was these which were the cause of the vile odour.

Soon the putrid corpses were piled high by the road-side, the marks of some leprous plague on their rotting hides. And everywhere were flies. Big, fat flies, gorging on the foul remains. It was like a battlefield — which had had knightly mules and proud pigs as its participants, instead of men. The further Tallow went, the more he wanted to vomit as the number of corpses increased. Once or twice he saw a human corpse, bloated, putrid and bearing the signs of the same disease as the animals.

Tallow debated whether it was wise to continue. The plague which had killed so many was a thing to be avoided. But the child was not his responsibility. He could only go on — in his boat it would hamper his progress.

The grey thatch of cottages lay ahead and smoke hung over it, clinging like an obscene bat to the area which the village occupied. For a mile, it seemed, there were only varying shades of grey. The village was bereft of colour. The nearer Tallow came to the place, the louder became the crackling of fire, the more pungent the smell of burnt flesh.

He recalled the witch-burnings of his boyhood. Yes, the smell was familiar. But screams and laughter were not apparent. Obviously the witch was roasted, if, of course. witch it was who blazed.

92

Hovering on the outskirts of the village, shifting from one foot to the other, Tallow attempted to peer through the death-laden smoke, but it was impossible to make much out. He could see nothing but a flicker of fire and a few moving shapes in the murk. The sound of men walking and the grunt of human voices told him that the village was inhabited.

Reassured, he continued his way towards the fire. All around him rose the walls of cottages, menacing sentinels.

Then he saw them. Tattered skeletons moving near the fire, and then drawing back from it, like a tide. They flung burdens on to the fire.

Tallow shivered; the stench of death was everywhere, fouling the atmosphere. As he neared the skeleton figures, one turned and saw him. Tallow was nauseated, there seemed hardly a shred of flesh on the man — yet he lived. Blotches of green, mauve and yellow spattered their way over his face. Only his eyes were dark — staring out of holes in his skull.

"What do you want?" said the man hollowly.

"I have brought a child I found in the forest. It was abandoned."

"Take it away — and leave while you can."

"But I cannot keep it."

"Neither can we."

"Surely there's a woman here who'll take it in."

"No."

"There must be."

"There is no woman who can spare food for a stranger-child."

"Are you the head man of the village?"

"No."

"Then I want to see him."

"He is dead."

"Did he die of the plague?"

"No. He starved to death."

"If the baby remains with me, it will starve also. Surely

you don't want that."

"I can do nothing about it."

Tallow jerked his way through the staring villagers, going up to a woman; she looked at him apathetically.

"Will you take the baby?"

"No."

"Would you let a child starve?"

"My children have starved to death."

"This one will take their place."

"On the fire?"

Tallow looked desperately about him, ringed by dull skulls.

"Someone *must* take the baby!"

No answer.

"They *must*!"

The villagers turned away and began to throw more burdens on to the fire. Tallow saw that the burdens were corpses — flopping, skinny bodies.

"Where's the next village?"

A grey bone pointed westwards.

"Five miles."

"Wretches — pitiless horrors! May the plague take you all!"

Then Tallow fled westwards, running hard, the cradle like a boulder in his arms. The skeletons watched him leave and one of them smiled — a gaping split in his head.

Tallow did not pause until a hill obscured the village and he could only see the slowly rising smoke above it. Then he stopped for a moment, before resuming his trek westwards with long striding steps.

He felt bile in his throat and his thoughts were constantly upon the safety of the boat he had left miles back at the river-bank.

He knew he had reached the next village. The smoke hovering over a valley told him where to find it.

It was a larger village, with a larger fire and even fewer of the living-dead. Fire blazed on some rooftops, and houses crumbled. Two stark-eyed horses sped by bearing fleshless naked riders who held torches in their talons and flung flame wherever they passed.

Apart from the thumping hooves and the sound of fire, there was silence. It was as if the smoke was a cloak, muffling most noise.

Tallow plucked the child from its blanket and flung the cot upon a blazing heap of bodies. Then, with less weight to carry, he backed out of the village and loped towards the hills. He was frantic and furious. His luck had left him.

The child woke up and began to wail. Tallow quieted it by the simplest method he knew. He put his hand over its mouth. Such noise seemed sacrilege.

He coughed and spat a vile taste from his throat. As he ran on, the two riders galloped past him, racing one another up the valley slopes. Torches still flared in their hands and their ribs tore through their pale hides.

Humped over their steeds, they reached the top of the hill and disappeared. Tallow stumbled after them, hearing his own voice crying to them, but he could not hear the words.

For the rest of the day, Tallow scoured the miles which lay eastwards and westwards, and everywhere he saw smoke, sometimes riders, but he avoided them wherever possible. He could not stop the baby's crying, and soon he was no longer aware of it.

Tortured and torn, Tallow grew aimless. His mind was chaotic, his loneliness, never previously sensed, a terrible thing. The world took on proportions of towering fear and creeping horror and he felt he must be in Hell as he staggered over the dreadful countryside, the baby clutched to his chest. The child was linked to him by disturbing ties and he could not now be rid of it. There was no one to help him – no mother, no Miranda, no Mesmers. He was alone, completely, and could see no way out of the circumstances he had effected.

He had denied his mother, his lover and his teacher and,

95

lacking these, had taken a responsibility upon himself which he was incapable of accepting.

For the first time, the travesty became like one of his fellow human beings; a condition brought about by the combined influences of those he encountered on his trip down river. Again he experienced mental anguish and subjective emotion, but this time he did not fear it — he could not. It engulfed him.

Hemmed in by smoking villages and the horrors of famine and plague, he soon lost all sense of direction.

The hills were heaving mounds of green slime, waiting to smother him. The valleys were gaping maws waiting to gobble him. There was no escape, nowhere to hide. Nowhere to go.

Then the river flashed ahead. With a sob of thanks he ran towards it, reached it, wetted his aching head in it, embraced it; the child lying helpless beside him on the grass.

He ran upriver, anxiously scanning the bank for his boat. He found it where he'd left it. An old wizened man stood near it, regarding it through benevolent eyes. His face was shielded by a battered, broad-brimmed hat and he smiled amiably at Tallow as he approached. Seeing the man, Tallow was reminded of the baby he had left further down.

"A baby," he said. "Down there." He pointed. The old man's benevolence and amiability, at close quarters, was the outward sign of his senility, for he only grinned and nodded at Tallow.

"Do you understand?" asked Tallow abruptly.

"Yeth," replied the old man through a mouth devoid of teeth, wet and wrinkled.

"Will you look after it?"

"Yeth." But he did not move.

"You're sure?"

"Yeth."

Tallow boarded his boat and cast off. The man on the bank remained still, smiling at Tallow, his eyes dim and blank.

"You're sure?"

The wizened ancient had turned away.

"You're sure?" Tallow called after him, but he didn't hear the shout.

Tallow soulfully started the motor; it throbbed angrily, turning the propeller, churning the water.

In a few moments, he had gone past the wailing child and was on his way down-river again.

Chapter Thirteen

TALLOW REGARDED THE MEN BLEAKLY, fatalistically. It was two days since he had left the place of the smoking villages. He accepted the fact that he was to be delayed again and hoped that it would be for only a short time.

He had been waylaid by the ruffians as he rested on the bank beside the boat. There were bearded and garbed in the remnants of uniforms, originally of some neutral colour which had been obscured by grime. Their lean hands were moulded around guns — pistols and rifles.

"What do you want? I've nothing of value — and I need my boat," said Tallow sadly.

"We want your boat," answered the foremost, grinning a wolf's grin. "And information."

"I need my boat, and I have no information of use to you."

"Where are you from?"

"Many towns up-river."

"Where are you bound?"

"I don't know."

"You don't know? You don't know where you're going? Then why are you so anxious to keep your boat?"

"I am following another ship. A great golden barge — perhaps you've seen it pass?"

"We've seen no craft of the sort you describe. *We* need your boat. Let's not have to shoot you. Join us or die." He rattled off the last sentence in the same way as a hungry child rattles off grace.

"But —"

"It's your choice, friend. We've little time to waste."

"I'll join you," said Tallow hastily. "But what am I joining?"

"Zhist's Army. The Free Fighters."

Tallow whimpered under his breath. "I'll join," he said. "I'll join any army of men fighting for freedom. Yes, indeed, the prospect arouses the old fire in my heart. What do you want me to do, comrade?"

The soldier smirked cynically at Tallow. "Let us make use of your boat," he said.

"Certainly," assented Tallow. "It is yours."

"I know," grinned the soldier. Then he said: "You can help us load the crates."

Tallow was escorted back into the bushes. Here were more men of the same stamp, sitting on long wooden boxes, like coarse coffins. They all had the appearance of carnivores which had been fed on fruit for months. They were lean, fox-featured and half-starved. Some of them got up as Tallow and the others entered the clearing.

"This the boatman?" growled one of them, jerking his thumb at Tallow.

"Yes — he's joined us. We'll have to have him vetted by Zhist, of course. But that'll be later. Meanwhile, he loads with us — and drives that boat."

"Very well, let's get started."

Tallow lifted one end of a crate and the speaker took the

other. They staggered with it to the boat. The man made to heave it on, but Tallow stopped him.

"I'll supervise the stacking," he said. "You could capsize her by doing that."

The soldier looked at his leader, questioningly. The leader nodded. Tallow skipped aboard and began to check the loading.

Soon the boat was low in the water, heavy with crates. The leader joined Tallow in the small cabin. "Now," he said, "steer where I direct. It was lucky you came along. It would have taken days to have carted this lot overland. And we've no time to waste."

It took hours — and Tallow was forced to guide his boat into a smaller stream which joined the main river. This wound for miles inland.

Then they disembarked and pushed their way through thick near-tropical vegetation. Tallow had soon lost all his sense of direction but somehow the leader of the ambushers — Niko — appeared to know exactly where he was going.

They broke out into a clearing as the sun set. Thick with tents and shanties, it was smeared with sprawled bodies and tiny camp-fires. A few men stood around talking. Slatternly women cooked over fires and everywhere guns were stacked against the sides of the makeshift shacks and tents.

"This way," instructed Niko, leading Tallow towards a shack, larger than the rest, which occupied the centre of the clearing. He stopped and knocked on the side.

"Who is it?" The voice coming from the depths of the hut was low and vibrant, like a cat's purr.

"This is Niko. I've brought along a new recruit for you to have a look at — his name's Tallow. We commandeered his boat, Colonel Zhist."

"Enter."

The interior of the hut was dark and smelled predominantly of foul pipe-tobacco. When Tallow's eyes became accustomed to the darkness he saw a man only six inches taller than he. A short man with a thin fringe of beard, large brown eyes and a tight mouth dominated by an eagle's beak of a nose. His head was sharp and tapering, his body thin and wiry.

"Thanks, Niko, you can go," said Zhist, nodding to his lieutenant. "Tallow is a stranger here, is he not?" His voice was soft and precise.

"Yes, sir," replied Niko as he got up and ducked out of the shack.

When Niko had left, Zhist signed for Tallow to squat down beside him. He was puffing on a large pipe. He waved a pouch of tobacco at Tallow who accepted it and stuffed his own pipe full of the thick, coarse stuff. He lit up, the smoke boiling into his throat. He coughed, his whole body shaking as the stuff reached his lungs.

"Not used to our forest blend, obviously," smiled Zhist.

"No," said Tallow, reassured by Zhist's friendly manner. "What do you want to ask me about?"

"I want to find out whether you're a spy — whether you'll be useful to us. Whether you can be trusted."

Tallow decided to risk frankness. "I'm not a spy," he said. "I don't know whether I'll be useful to you and you can trust me not to betray any of your plans — but you cannot trust me to remain with you if I get a real chance to go on my way — I have an urgent mission."

"Fair enough," said Zhist. "You owe us nothing. But let me tell you a little of what we're fighting for — then maybe you'll be more sympathetic to our cause."

"Very well," assented Tallow, "but I warn you — much of what you say will be lost on me."

"I'll risk that," said Zhist gravely. "We're outlaws — renegades — guerillas. A number of other names, according to where your sympathies lie. Seven years ago our ruler, Prince Gorlin, was deposed by the people. He wasn't a bad man — it was simply that he represented a system of government which was decadent, uneconomic, unjust and outdated. So we changed it, banished Gorlin and set up a new system of government temporarily controlled by the man who had led the revolution, General Damaiel Natcho. Is it inevitable, what happened? Natcho abused the trust the people had put in him. He imposed a more tyrannical rule upon the people than Gorlin's ministers had ever done and, since most of the army consisted of men who admired and respected Natcho, he managed to keep the people down. Many of them, me included, attempted to rouse our countrymen to overthrow him. This failed. A number of us were captured, shot — others, like me, fled to the woodlands. Since then we have been fighting Natcho when we could and slowly building up our own army. I am certain he doesn't know how well organised we are. Otherwise he might well have defeated us by a concerted attack at any time. We are a thorn in his side, but one which he has underestimated. Recently we raided an army arsenal and escaped with most of the guns stored there. We blew the place up afterwards and made it appear that the guns had been destroyed with the buildings. Now we are well-armed and are ready to attack Rimsho, our capital city, and depose Natcho."

In his dirty cap and uniform, ragged of beard and of speech, Conrad Zhist had not much to inspire men to follow him. Not at first sight, anyway. As he crouched in the gloomy shack and murmured his plans and his reasons for making them to Tallow, then it became apparent why. Zhist was an orator; a natural orator with a gift for picking words which, in their very sounds, were keyed to the pitch of men's emotions. It was not his lucid choice of phrases which made him what he was — it was his onomatopoeic flare of rhetoric, the rough, inspiring music of his voice. Tallow soon found himself listening to the rhythms rather than to the sentences, his various emotions being triggered off by certain words and phrases which, combined, made him feel that the only thing in the world he wanted was a rifle — the only enemy Damaiel Natcho.

By the time Zhist had finished, Tallow was thinking of

ways and means to help him, all his earlier urgency to reach the golden barge forgotten. Zhist had probably known this before he began talking, had relied on his talents to win Tallow as an ally.

Now Tallow was speaking, quickly, excitedly.

"With my boat, you will be able to keep in closer liason with many of your men. I will be able to steer it, and you can ride in it with me. We can travel up and down the rivers, gathering recruits. What do you say?"

"I like the idea," smiled Zhist. "You're ready to change what you said earlier, are you?"

"Yes," said Tallow. "Yes — you can trust me, Colonel. I'm your man."

"Good." Zhist sat back, puffing on his pipe with an air of satisfaction. "I'll fix you up with quarters — and a gun."

Tallow didn't like the sound of his having a gun. He had no experience of fire-arms, but he didn't object when Zhist took him outside, picked up a rifle and handed it to him.

"Know how to check the firing mechanism and ammunition?"

"No," said Tallow.

"I'll get someone to show you. Hang on to that gun — and never lose sight of it. It's precious."

"Thanks," murmured Tallow uneasily.

Zhist took him over to one of the many camp-fires. Three men sprawling around it got up and saluted as he reached them.

"This is Jephraim Tallow," Zhist said. "I want you to show him the ropes. He'll be kipping with you boys. Show him how to use that rifle he's got." He patted Tallow on the back and left the three soldiers staring at the little man with amusement and interest.

"That gun looks a bit big for you, mate." The shortest of the soldiers, a man about five-foot-six, grinned.

"It is, my friend," said Tallow, wary inside but seeming calm and self-possessed to the others. "But the bullets do as much damage as anyone's."

The three men laughed self-consciously. "Well," said the tallest, "since Zhist seems to like you — welcome to our camp. I'll show you where our tent is." Tallow turned his back on the other two and followed the man through a maze of fires and shacks to a large canvas tent. He stooped and entered. Inside it was littered with lengths of webbing, boots, haversacks, dirty plates and other equipment collected by encamped soldiers.

"Clear a space and put your gear on it," said the soldier. "My name's Jantor. Stay here, I'll get you a sleeping bag."

"That's good of you," said Tallow, "thanks a lot."

"Don't mention it," smirked Tallow's future billet mate, and he crawled out of the opening.

Tallow looked distastefully at the rubbish cluttering the ground and with his boot kicked away much of the stuff which did not lie on untidy sleeping-bags, making an oblong clearing in the refuse. By the time he had finished, Jantor returned with a rolled-up sleeping bag under his arm and dumped it down with a grunt.

"Here you are," he said. "Get settled in and join us for a game of cards later, if you like. We'll be at the fire."

"Thanks," said Tallow. He couldn't reach the man — couldn't manoeuvre him. It was demoralising. He decided not to join the card-game as he unrolled the bag, discovering as he did so, that at one end of it, where his head would be, a small mound he had thought would be useful as a pillow was, in fact an ant-hill.

Sighing, Tallow crawled into the bag and subsided into sleep.

Tallow remained in the camp three days, learning how to use a gun and meeting the men who were now his comrades-in-arms.

The revolutionaries were good men, every one of them — eyes perpetually bright in mud-grimed, bearded faces, their tattered uniforms kept together by leather straps bearing arms and ammunition. They were fighting mainly out of desperation. Originally they had talked politics and spoken high, idealistic phrases. Now they fought for their lives, their families — and they fought from habit; it kept them going. They would crawl through the forests on their bellies until it became second-nature to crawl, to keep a finger on a trigger, to talk in sparing whispers, to tread softly, carefully. And it was second nature for them to hate. They did that from habit, too — though they still had cause to hate — for Natcho had driven them out, destroyed their dreams. There was much that could be destroyed in men which they would accept, — dignity, love, loyalty — even their souls — but it was dangerous to kill dreams. Natcho would, said the men, soon realise that. In talks with Zhist, Tallow learned that the country controlled by Natcho was a nation of six million people. Next to it was a monarchy, larger but having fewer industries. It was mainly a rural country — lorded over by barons and dukes who, in turn, were lorded over by a king — a dull, stupid man who was controlled by his minsters. The ministers, the barons and the dukes all were envious of the industries of their neighbour and war had been frequent, down the centuries, between the two countries.

At the moment, Natcho was worried. The king, egged on by his ministers, was constantly raising his voice and shaking his fist towards the other country, crying that the land had been overrun by peasants who knew nothing of rulership and that he, personally, would one day see fit to restore a monarchy to the vacant throne. He did not state which monarchy. War was imminent and Natcho had to spend much time parleying with ambassadors. In this way, also, was his strength weakened.

Zhist, however, realised that even were he and his followers successful in deposing Natcho, they would have to guard against attack.

The day came when all the revolutionaries were marshalled in one place — Zhist's main camp where Tallow was billeted. Tallow was visited by Zhist and asked to accompany the Colonel to his quarters.

Again Zhist offered tobacco to Tallow and Tallow accepted. He was feeling miserable. He had been unable to become friendly with his three comrades and they had constantly made remarks about his puny size and awkwardness. Zhist's request came to him as a relief and for the first time since he had arrived in the camp, he managed to relax a little.

"I've become bored, Colonel," said Tallow. "Is there something for me to do at last?"

"Yes," replied Zhist, "there is. I want you to take me down-river — to a place about a mile away from the capital. I have scouts there and spies who will tell me the latest news of Natcho's movements. Have your boat ready to leave in a quarter-of-an-hour. I'll join you there."

Tallow got up quickly. "Depend on me," he sang as he ran out of the shack, towards the river.

They made the journey down-river safely, uneventfully, and on the bank were met by a party of soldiers, Niko amongst them, who swiftly helped them ashore.

"There's a carnival in the city," said Niko, his mouth twitching. "A red, blue and yellow affair with roundabouts and side shows. Haven't seen one since I was a kid!"

A carnival in Rimsho? What's Natcho's game?"

"I'd say he smelled trouble and has brought the carnival in to lull the people. The whole city's in confusion and everyone's going to the carnival. The sideshows are outside the suburbs — on the Big Green where we used to hold our sports."

"I know it," said Zhist laconically. "This is a break for us. Many of us can join the crowds and assemble well inside the city. There are strangers in town — gypsies — so bearded face and wary walk won't be so noticeable."

"You expect to be able to penetrate the city disguised as fair-folk?" said Tallow aghast. "But how will you hide your guns?"

"We'll only take pistols," Zhist told him. "We'll get any

106

rifles we need from members of Natcho's army." He paused and slapped Tallow on the back. "Tallow, my friend," he sighed. "You may not know it, but this is the opportunity I've needed. Fate is on our side today."

"But what do you hope to achieve apart from your own suicide?" said Tallow.

"We'll be able to rouse the people. They are all sick of Natcho's rule. The carnival is a relief from it, true, but not enough to make them insensitive to years of oppression. Also, we'll be able to save innocent lives by warning those incapable of fighting to stay in their homes until peace is restored."

"What do I do?" asked Tallow, dreading to hear the answer.

"You can guard the boat and do what you can in this area. When the city's won, I'll send for you. You may not know much of fighting, Tallow; but you've got a brain. And something else. Something, I think, which I once had and lost to some degree. I should hope that there'll be a place for you in civil administration when we get organised; that's if you want it, of course. We'll have to work fast — for Hyriom lurks at our borders even now, with loaded guns, eager for civil war and a weakened nation."

Tallow breathed in relief. "I'll wait here, then," he smiled. "Good luck."

"Thanks," said Zhist as he led his men back into the forest.

Chapter Fourteen

MIRANDA WAS SURPRISED to see the bustle and commotion in the city. She had been warned by the captain of the ship that she might find it dull and restrictive. On the contrary, it appeared to be a city gone mad with colour and cacophony. Hurdy-gurdies blared out their brassy music, tradesmen called their wares, and stall-vendors bellowed the delights of their games and prizes.

"So this is Rimsho, is it?" She spoke to her escort, the young sailor, Cannfer. "It must have changed a good deal since you put in here last."

"It has, darling. Never thought I'd see it. The old bastard who used to control the city must be dead or deposed." Cannfer stared over the thronged quayside. "No!" he exclaimed, surprised. "There's his picture — big as a house, pasted on that far wall. See it?" He pointed.

Miranda saw a painting of a handsome, grey-haired, military-looking man. "Sexy," she said.

Cannfer grinned. "I'm jealous," he said. "Before I know it, you'll be after him!"

Miranda became serious. "Remember what I told you," she frowned. "Remember — never get jealous. One day I may find my lover Jephraim again."

Cannfer looked at the ground. "I'll remember."

Miranda took his hand. "Come on," she smiled. "Let's join in the fun."

Zhist, lurking in the shade of a red and black striped booth, saw Miranda and Cannfer disembark. He craned his head in order to see if others were coming ashore, but the girl and the sailor were the only ones.

Zhist had hoped that the entire crew of the ship would go ashore, then he and a few of his men might have sneaked aboard and stolen whatever arms there were. Although disappointed, he still regarded Miranda and her escort with interest. Always anxious for information, he decided that he would talk to them as soon as he could. As they mingled with the holiday-makers, he slipped from his hiding-place and followed them.

Tallow, for all his relief that he did not have to risk the dangers of the town, soon became bored with waiting. In his cabin was a flask of rum. Thoughts of boredom were quickly gone; all coherent thoughts, in fact, disappeared. Tallow finished the flask and collapsed, happily, to the ground. He lay with a seraphic smile on his ugly features, looking more like a contented crocodile than anything else.

He slept and dreamed of a dragon with a hundred eyes which moved relentlessly towards him. He was armed with a green sword which flashed with some slumbering power, which gave him strength and a mysterious grandeur. The dragon bore down on him. Behind it lurked huge-boled trees which had their topmost branches hidden by a dense layer of gleaming, deep-blue clouds. The trees were orange and yellow and the dragon was black with diamond eyes. Its red-fanged mouth was wide

109

and a long tongue flickered out. It touched Tallow and the sword-power flowed through him, healing a wound the poisonous tongue had made. He hacked at the tongue and the thing flopped to the ground to wriggle away into the undergrowth.

Then, in his dream, the dragon swallowed Tallow. Breathed him in, down into the maw, down into the stomach which was lighted by torches of black-flame.

The sword was gone from Tallow's aching hand and he travelled downwards into the dragon with incredible velocity. So fast was he going that soon he could make out nothing but a blur on both sides and utter darkness ahead. He began to scream and then he woke up.

Zhist and Miranda stood over him. Miranda looked vaguely uncomfortable and Zhist frowned.

Tallow was certain that he was not awake; he believed that he had simply switched dreams. He lay on his back, waiting for something to happen.

Zhist grunted: "I hadn't expected this, Tallow. I think that the lady here knows you."

Tallow struggled to a sitting posture.

"Yes," he said, eyeing Miranda warily. "We have met."

"I've found you, Jephraim," said Miranda softly. "I'm glad. I'm sorry if what happened was my fault. I forgive you."

"Thanks," Tallow winced as he got to his feet. His head felt delicate and his hands shook. "How did you find me?"

"Colonel Zhist mentioned your name. We're going to help him win his revolution."

"We?"

"Cannfer and I. Don't worry, darling, he knows about our relationship. I've told him not to be jealous."

"Good," lied Tallow, wondering how he could get out of this situation. "How do you intend to help Colonel Zhist?"

"I'm going to seduce President Natcho, keep him busy while the Colonel takes the city."

Tallow decided not to continue his questioning. "I see,"

110

he said after a while.

"Come on, Jephraim." Zhist motioned tersely. "We'll need your help. We're going back into the city. The revolution begins tonight. We want you and Miranda to berth in Rimsho and ask to see the President. Then you'll get a message to him that you have a girl for sale. Such deals are frequent under Natcho's regime."

Tallow was in no position to resist. He said: "Very well, Colonel, we'll get going now, shall we?"

"Yes," replied Zhist. "But don't let me down."

"I shan't, Colonel," said Tallow as he started the motor and helped Miranda aboard without meeting her eyes.

Neither Miranda nor Tallow attempted to begin a conversation and the journey to Rimsho was completed in silence. They berthed half-an-hour after leaving Zhist. Tallow hailed an urchin who chewed grubby candy-floss, dangling his legs over the oily water.

"You!" shouted Tallow. "Tell one of the President's guards that I have a message for His Excellency."

The boy blinked, then he scurried off. He soon reappeared, pointing Tallow out to a brown-uniformed soldier. The man came up to Tallow's boat and saluted politely.

"You have a message for President Natcho?"

"That's right," said Tallow, assuming a crafty air, "I have a personal letter for him."

"I will have it delivered," assured the soldier.

Tallow handed it to him. The soldier saluted again and strode off into the crowd.

Tallow and Miranda had to wait for another half-hour before the soldier returned.

"The President orders me to accompany you to his palace," said the soldier, saluting again.

Tallow and Miranda disembarked from the boat and followed the man through the jostling populace of Rimsho.

Tallow did not like the faces of the people. Their grins

111

were too fixed. Brittle smiles and uneasy laughter. Their eyes were glassy and bewildered. They had been too long under Natcho's heel to remember how to be happy. They could not see the enjoyment and freedom lasting; this festival was a respite, not an escape. Despair and darkness was behind them, oppression and fear ahead of them. Most of them were drunk; many of them were near to collapsing, but they carried on drinking, not daring to stop. They were pitiful, these people, but Tallow felt only contempt for them.

He felt uncomfortable and dazed. Very little of the happenings of the immediate past had affected his brain. He could not register what he felt — nor could he accept Miranda's presence. She was there and he knew he wasn't dreaming, yet he could not get close to her, could think of nothing to say. He wished that he were back on the wooded bank of the river — anywhere but in Rimsho with Miranda by his side. Soon they were walking in quieter streets — a larger bleak building ahead of them, squat dwellings on either side. On top of the big building was a flag which Tallow recognised as one which Zhist had described to him. It was green with a black falcon emblazoned upon it. Natcho's flag. They came to the end of the street and passed through guarded gates, mounting a long, wide flight of stone steps. A huge doorway was black and unwelcoming. They entered it and Miranda and Tallow were left in the centre of a vast corridor while the soldier showed some papers to a guard and talked with him for a few minutes. The soldier returned to them and motioned for them to precede him down the corridor. At the end of the corridor was another guard and the soldier once more showed his papers and held a short whispered conversation. The guard opened the big metal doors and said loudly:

"Corporal Blight and party."

A gruff voice, softened by a slight echo, said: "Enter."

The soldier led Tallow and Miranda into a large hall devoid of ornament. It was a naked hall, furnished only by a big desk at the far end. At the desk sat a big man, older than the man whose portraits decorated the city but obviously President Natcho. He had small eyes and an upper lip which folded down over his lower lip. His moustache was grey and short, a military moustache. A fuzz of grey hair on his chin attempted to strengthen it and hide the folds of flesh beneath it but it only served to emphasise weakness and age. Natcho was dressed in a simple brown military uniform and wore a cap upon his grey head. Several medals adorned the right breast of his tunic and he sat with his hands folded in front of him, staring sternly at his visitors.

"You may leave us now, Blight," he said.

Blight saluted, clicked his heels, wheeled sharply about and left the hall, closing the metal doors behind him.

"This is the girl?" Natcho enquired abstractedly, eyeing Miranda with a dispassionate appraisal which made her feel the need to vomit.

"Yes, your Excellency."

"How much?"

"Thirty gold pieces," recited Tallow, remembering the little Zhist had told him.

"Good. I'll give you a note to my secretary. He'll pay you your money. Is the girl clean?"

"Yes, Your Excellency."

"She'd better be," growled Natcho. On his desk was a bottle of brandy and a large glass. He poured brandy into the glass, drank it down in a gulp, winced and held his stomach with his left hand. His eyes had pain in them as he motioned Tallow to leave.

"The note, Your Excellency?"

The eyes were suddenly angry and Tallow regretted the insistence in his tone. Then the expression faded from the President's face and he opened a drawer and took out paper, pen and ink. He scribbled something down, folded the note and held it out. Tallow ran up to take it, then, with a peculiar glance at Miranda, walked swiftly past her and opened the doors.

Outside, he asked the guard: "Where do I find the President's Secretary?"

"Upstairs," replied the guard. "First door on your right."

Tallow scampered up the stairs the guard indicated and located the door. He knocked. A bored and languid voice drawled, "Come in."

Tallow entered the room. It was much smaller than the hall he had just left but almost as bare. Save for a filing cabinet which stood near a window overlooking a courtyard, and a desk and chair, it had no furnishings.

A bland-faced and elegant young man was sitting on the edge of the desk lighting a long-stemmed pipe. He raised an eyebrow when he saw Tallow and stared at the little man in affected amusement. "What can I do for you — sir," he said, insolently and indolently.

"Are you the President's Secretary?" Tallow was feeling increasingly uncomfortable.

"I am."

"I have a note for you."

The languid Secretary stretched out his hand and Tallow put the letter into it.

Placing his pipe carefully in a narrow oblong ash-tray, the Secretary dusted down his spotless uniform with delicate fingers and unfolded the note. He studied it for some moments, refolded it, placed it on his desk and put a heavy gold paper-weight on top of it.

"I see," he drawled mysteriously, looking Tallow up and down lazily. "Wait here, will you?"

"Yes," said Tallow, his fingers curling and anger flowing through him. He did not have to wait very long. Almost immediately the Secretary returned with two burly guards. He pointed at Tallow. "Take him to the cell-block," he commanded. "Keep him there until you receive further orders."

Tallow felt panic. "What have I done?" he shouted,

114

struggling between the two guards. "Why are you arresting me?"

"President's orders, old boy," smiled the Secretary sadly. "That's what the note suggested — that you be arrested."

"But why?"

"Don't ask me," the Secretary answered wistfully as if Tallow had been granted a great honour which the Secretary coveted. "You may discover that later."

Tallow was pushed roughly into the corridor and borne through long corridors, down stairs, into another corridor lined with barred doors. One of these was opened and he was shoved into a concrete cell, windowless and dark. A light bulb illuminated the cell and the place was shadowless. A narrow wooden bench occupied one side of the cell.

For the second time, Tallow became a prisoner, only this time his gaolers made no secret of his status.

An hour later Miranda joined him in the cell. A guard laughed as he pushed her in and said something unintelligible.

"What happened?" said Tallow dully.

"Natcho knew something of our plan," she said abstractedly, staring at the wall. "He knew that you are in Zhist's employ, at least. Apparently he had a spy in Zhist's camp at the time you joined the rebels. The man obviously discovered little, for Zhist did not trust him, then. But your description and the circumstances under which you joined Zhist were well known to Natcho. He intends to torture us in order to find out about Zhist's plans."

"I felt that there was something wrong," said Tallow moodily. "I couldn't tell what, but I knew it. Has Natcho any idea of when the new revolution begins?"

"No — and he certainly doesn't expect it so soon. There may be a chance for us yet. We may be liberated before he begins his tortures."

"I hope so," said Tallow, feelingly. "Though I doubt it. I am not a lucky man."

"No." Miranda considered this. "You are not lucky.

115

There is a doom about you, Jephraim and I cannot tell what it is — I wish I knew. Then I might help you."

"I do not need anyone's help!" Tallow snorted. "But I am weary of interference. I wish only to be left in peace to pursue my destiny in my own way. Too many people have interfered already — you most of all, for I welcomed your interference at first. I did not wish to dispose of you in the way I did — but I had to. For my sake mainly, but also for yours. There is no great happiness in my fate, Miranda. There is nothing but doom. But I shall welcome the doom when it comes. I would not wish to involve anyone else."

"Suppose someone else wishes to become involved?" whispered Miranda softly.

"Then I will eventually destroy them. Not out of hate, you understand, but out of necessity. I do not wish to destroy — but it is a question of survival. I cannot be hampered. I still love you, Miranda, I think, but this does not alter the fact that I cannot take you with me. You have contributed much to my downfall. And I to yours, I suppose."

"That cannot be rectified now, my love," said Miranda, "but can't we see that the future is better?"

"How can I tell? The future is unknown to me. I have staked my soul upon the future — and I cannot share what is ahead. My quest is for something so intangible that I cannot even feel it properly — let alone describe it. I seek for something I lack — yet the more I seek the more I lose of myself. Even those I have destroyed in some ways have, in turn, destroyed part of me — they have made my quest more and more difficult. I have only a faint hope that I can resume my journey. I must discover what I seek before I die, otherwise I am lost."

"You need help," said Miranda simply, with conviction. "You need my help, Jephraim — and you need the help of men like Zhist."

"No!' I need no help but my own. I am tormented by those who attempt to help me. I have never required their help

— never asked it. I wish to be left alone. I wish for my own dark peace — not the black agony which comes with friendship and responsibility. I am forced too often to make decisions which should be unnecessary. I am not like other men — I am not greater than they are, neither am I smaller — I am apart from them and they try to make me like them. This can never be. Humanity does not admit Tallow into its ranks and Tallow has no ambition to join humanity. I am separate as I have always been. When I meet men I like, I conflict with them, ruin them as they ruin me. I have no place among you — and I need no friends or lovers for they only become my enemies, and I theirs. I cannot argue with them, I cannot fight them. Only men with something in common can conflict in this way. I have nothing to offer — and they can give me nothing."

"You speak of a soul," interjected Miranda. "If you have a soul — then you have something in common with us. You have made these barriers because you fear us — you fear our humanity! You are fighting your destiny in refusing to see this. Every man's destiny is to become absorbed — to lose that which makes him an individual. When he dies, his body is absorbed into the earth — his soul into the myriad souls of the world. You are no different at this moment. Break this link if you like, Jephraim. Break it if you can — but it will mean your complete destruction! You seek for something on earth which most men find in death. Your quest is for death — not life."

"You are *wrong* — utterly wrong! What I shall find will make death known to me — I shall not fear it. This is what makes me different — and apart from you and the rest."

Tallow was trembling, dizzy; he sat down, hunched on the bench, his long fingers clasped together, his whole body tight.

"Where does the river lead?" he said to himself.

Miranda knew that he had not asked her the question, but in spite of this she replied: "It leads to the sea — and all our souls are only the tiny drops from the sea."

He did not hear her, nor did he wish to. He shut himself

117

off from her and she knew that it was hopeless to continue.

They remained silent until the guards came for them several hours later. They had had no sign that the revolution had begun and Miranda was suddenly aware that it might have failed already. Until then, she had no thought of failure.

Eventually Tallow felt no more pain. Natcho's torturers were not subtle. They relied on the lash and the rack — and Miranda's screaming presence. They knew from previous experience that to torture a man's woman in front of him often loosened his tongue. But they did not know Tallow.

Miranda had been lashed and her body stretched until she had become a blind animal, a frenzied thing which bellowed for respite from the agony inflicted upon it and Tallow had sat watching — motionless, his eyes troubled but insensitive to her anguish; if he could hardly understand his own pain, how could he understand another's? Even when they had started on him — *lash, question, lash, question* — he had felt the pain in an abstract way, not fully knowing why he should suffer it. Only this had stopped him from answering the questions. It was not courage which had made him silent — he had not heard the questions. The Secretary's cool voice had become incorporated into the lash so that it was only part of it, like the swish before the sting.

His back was raw and his bones ached horribly. His body throbbed and he moaned in agony. Soon, he gasped when he moved, when the lash fell, but he gasped because he knew his body was in pain, though he no longer felt it.

At last the Secretary said wearily: "Take them back to their cell. I did not realise that human beings could be so tenacious. They might as well be animals, unable to speak our tongue. All they can do is whine for mercy — and tell us nothing of what they know. They puzzle me." He motioned distastefully to the guards and left the torture room. Then suddenly he was back again.

118

"On second thoughts," he said, "release them. And have them followed by our best tracker. They may lead us to a den of their fellows. The more we have in our net — the more chance we'll have of finding out about their plans."

A guard with the face of a moose nodded and hauled Tallow and Miranda up. Both were naked and bleeding, their blood mingling, their breath in unison.

The moose grunted to another soldier who picked Miranda from the blood-spattered stone floor and flung her over his shoulder. The pair left the room by a different door, one which led downwards into a dark, unlighted tunnel. They tramped for two miles along this tunnel until, at last, they came to another door. This led out on to a part of the forest which crouched near the western wall of the city. The place had been fenced off. It was a burial ground. Open graves had been dug and filled with quick-lime. A few decaying corpses lay in the graves. The guards passed these and unlocked a small gate in the fence. They took the man and the woman some distance into the forest and dropped them to the ground, then they returned, introspectively picking droplets of dried blood off their uniforms.

Later, in grey twilight, Miranda recovered consciousness and pulled herself painfully into a sitting position. Tallow lay nearby; he had not yet awakened. Miranda crawled slowly towards him, every movement sending fresh spurts of agony through her ruined body.

Around her and above her the trees of the forest seemed to seethe with sentience — with malevolent life. They were the oldest, tallest trees she had ever seen, and their trunks twisted skywards to be lost to her vision. Tallow, face down in the moss, mumbled in quiet delirium. Miranda tenderly rolled him over and saw that his eyes were wide and blank, the irises small, the orbs rolling wildly.

A slight scuffling in the undergrowth behind her attracted her attention. She turned round and winced as the movement

119

sent new pain through her. She stared into the gloom but could see nothing which could have caused the kind of sound she had heard. There was only blackness beyond the first circle of ancient trees.

She returned her attention to Tallow who now looked at her in puzzlement. "Miranda?" he mouthed through lips which were puffed and blue.

"Don't worry, darling," she said. "It seems they have released us."

"We're free?"

"Yes, love."

"Why — ?"

"Because we could not talk, I suppose. We must find water. Can you get up?"

Tallow rose to his feet and shrieked as the lash-wounds burned into him. "God!" he swore. "Why did they do this to us?"

"For information."

"But we gave it to them didn't we — how did we bear this? I must have told them what they wanted."

"You did not — and I don't know why. I knew little and said less — but my motives, I suppose, were loyalty. You have no loyalty, save to yourself."

"You are right." He cringed as he tried to walk. "I cannot understand it. I must get back to my boat."

"Not yet, love, not yet. We should find a stream first and bathe our wounds."

She took his hands and slowly led him through the forest. Griff, the Tracker, lurking in the shadows of the big trees, craned his long neck and silently pecked his lips together. Griff had the sharp eyes of the bird of prey and he looked a little like the falcon which decorated Natcho's flag. Griff grinned to himself; there would be no difficulty in following these two for they could only travel slowly. The woods afforded all the cover he needed — more than enough. He slunk after the pair, silently;

120

as softly as a carrion bird.

Then they vanished. Baffled, Griff increased his pace and began to run lightly through the forest. It was darker now, but his eyes could see in the dark. His sharp ears could no longer hear the sound of their movements; they had disappeared completely. Griff was not superstitious, he was not imaginative enough to fear the supernatural for he was unaware of its possible existence. One moment they had been in sight, the next they were gone. Griff found their tracks and, with his face close to the ground, bent like a macabre ostrich, he traced the tracks until they, too, disappeared abruptly. Griff looked upwards into the trees and could not see them; he searched the ground around the last of the tracks and could find no tunnel or hollow into which they might have fallen.

Tallow and Miranda noticed nothing strange; they were both in too much pain to see that the forest was brighter and that the trees were of abnormal colours. Hand in hand, they searched for a river and finally found one, which was clear and pure. Thankfully, Miranda sank down beside the narrow stream and bathed her hands and head in it. Tallow collapsed beside her and lay, breathing heavily, on his stomach, his head pillowed by his claw-like hands.

The water soothed Miranda more than she had expected and it did the same for Tallow. After drinking of the stream they felt fitter and less weary. By now it was pitch dark and they could see little, not even the sky for it was obscured by a thick mesh of branches and leaves. They wandered on for a while, aimlessly, until they grew tired, a tiredness which was normal from lack of sleep, not the dreadful weariness of bodies which have borne torture. They slept and, upon awakening in the pale morning, were astounded at what they saw.

"Are we dead?" said Miranda, frowning at the orange-boled trees and the mauve leaves. "Or have we travelled into fairyland?"

"We are not dead," answered Tallow with confidence, "or

else I would know. And having had no experience of fairyland I cannot tell whether we are there or not, though I doubt it. Certainly the colourings of the vegetation are unusual, but there is probably a rational scientific explanation to the phenomenon. There is no law which says that bark should be brown and leaves green, is there? Or do we just expect them to be that way? We wouldn't be surprised if someone we knew who normally wore red clothing one day appeared in yellow clothes, so why should we be surprised by orange trunks and mauve leaves?"

"You are too logical, Jephraim," said Miranda slowly. "Far too logical to be human — if you really mean what you say. However, it's certainly reassuring to have your logic here. The place is very strange."

"I'm glad that you grant me one thing I said yesterday," grinned Tallow. "You said I was far too logical to be human. I don't know about the logic — but you've agreed, without realising it, that I'm not like the rest of humanity."

"All the more reason for you to strive to be like us," Miranda frowned. She got up and was surprised that the pain of the previous day was now only a dull ache. Tallow's back which had been red and raw was almost healed. "There's magic or something here," she said softly.

"Impossible!" Tallow exclaimed angrily. "The river we bathed in could be full of natural salts which we'd just not heard of before. I'll believe in magic when I see someone stop the sun rotating."

Miranda said nothing. She went up to one of the orange boles and examined it. Apart from its colour, it was the same as any other tree she had ever seen. "I suppose we'd better get moving," she said.

"All right," agreed Tallow, also studying the tree. "Which way?"

"Onwards, I suppose. If we got back we might well be captured again." She took his hand and led him forward over short grass which was bright yellow and cool to their naked feet.

The forest was cool also, even though the sun had reached its zenith and was glaring down through parts of the foliage less thick than the rest. There was an air of timelessness about the place, of ancient calm. Tallow's logic could not explain the alien sensations which came to him, the smell of the forest which was not quite like any other smell he knew. The bird-calls and the tiny golden birds which he saw from time to time were also unfamiliar.

"I wish I knew how long we were unconscious," he said, "perhaps we were taken to some foreign land — an island, possibly. I don't know why Natcho should go to that amount of trouble — but it looks as if that's what he did."

"It's the only explanation," agreed Miranda. "But there's something — unearthly — about the place. Something so calm and peaceful that it would seem we were on another planet."

"That's going a bit too far," said Tallow. "Almost like your idea that we're in fairyland!"

"I didn't mean that literally," Miranda said petulantly. "I only meant that it *seemed* like the fairyland I used to have described to me when I was a little girl."

"That seems to fit into your impression." Tallow smiled, pointing ahead. Miranda saw a vast domed building, manificent in marble and blue mosaic. It stood in a clearing of yellow grass and the marble caught the sun, flashing like fire. Miranda sighed. "We *must* still be dreaming," she said. "There's nothing else to explain it."

Both of them, in their own ways, were attempting to rationalise the place in which they found themselves. Both of them were trying to link it with things within their own experience. But it was virtually impossible.

They neared the domed construction and saw that it was supported by big marble columns set into a platform of milky jade. In the centre of the platform, a stairway of blue-stone curved upwards and disappeared into a circular aperture. There

123

were wide windows set into the sides of the raised building but they could not see inside. There were no inhabitants visible and it would have seemed strange to the pair if there had been. They crossed the yellow glade and stepped onto the green platform. It was warm, as if it had been exposed to the sun. Their unshod feet were helpful in their progress towards the stairway; if they had been wearing shoes, they would have slipped on the smooth stone.

They reached the blue steps and mounted them, staring upwards, but they could still see nothing. They did not attempt to ask themselves why they were invading the building with such assurance; it seemed quite natural that they should do what they were doing. There was no alternative.

Inside was a cool, shadowy hall, a blend of soft darkness and bright sunlight which entered by the windows. The floor was pearl-pink and the ceiling deep scarlet. The hall reminded Miranda of a womb. "It's wonderful," she breathed. "Magnificent!"

"Very pleasant," commented Tallow. "Certainly a change from the places I've been used to. I wonder who lives here."

"We may find out if we remain much longer," said Miranda. "The owners of this place may resent us entering it."

"Maybe," Tallow said, "but since there are no locks or even doors, I shouldn't be surprised if they aren't used to people coming in."

"Probably you're right."

Partially hidden by deep shadow was a small doorway and beyond it steps. Tallow looked questioningly at Miranda. "Do we proceed in our exploration?"

"We might as well."

They climbed the steps and found themselves in a smaller hall similar to the one beneath them. This hall, however, was furnished with twelve wide thrones placed in a semi-circle in the centre. Against the wall near the door were several chairs, upholstered in purple fabric. The thrones were of gold, decorated with fine silver, padded with white cloth. There was nothing barbaric or distasteful about the colours; they were quiet, blending with each other.

A door behind the thrones opened and a tall, fragile-looking man appeared, followed by others whose faces were almost identical. Only their robes were different in any notice-able way. Their faces were pale, almost white, their noses straight, their lips thin but not cruel. Their eyes were un-human — green-flecked eyes which stared into eternity with sad com-posure. The leader of the tall men looked at Tallow and Miranda. He nodded and waved a pale, long-fingered hand gracefully.

"Welcome," he said. His voice was high and frail, like a woman's, but beautiful in his modulation. The other eleven men seated themselves in the thrones but the first man, who had spoken, remained standing. "Sit down, please," he said.

Tallow and Miranda sat down on two of the purple chairs.

"How did you come here?" enquired the man. "Do you know?"

"No," replied Tallow, "we do not even know where we are."

"I thought not — your people rarely come to us, except by accident."

"Where are we?" asked Miranda as the man seated himself in the remaining throne.

"This is a place not *within* your own space-time continuum, yet *part* of it. There are strong links — though several dimensions separate us. Once our land was part of the earth you know, but in the dim past it became separated from the Mother Planet. Our bodies, unlike yours, are immortal. We choose this, but we are not bound to our flesh, as you are."

"I don't understand," frowned Tallow. "What are you saying?"

"I have said what I can in the simplest terms understandable to you. If you do not know what I say then I can explain no further. We are called, by some of your people who know of

125

us, guardians — though we guard nothing. We are warriors, if you like, fighting forces as alien to you as we are. We do not hate these forces, neither is there any material or ideological gain involved. We fight only to keep a balance of some kind."

"All very well," grunted Tallow. "But what has this to do with us?"

"Not much," admitted the man. "You came here by accident. We will attempt to get you back to your own continuum as soon as possible. Meanwhile you may stay here — or explore the surrounding forest, just as you like. You will not be harmed."

"Thanks," said Tallow, staring at Miranda. But the girl refused to look at him, her eyes were on the tall speaker.

"Can't we remain here?" she begged.

"No, you can not. One day, perhaps, many of you will join us. But that will be on what you call the day of judgement — or Armageddon. When your people are ready, long deaths and lives in the future of your plane, then shall we all assemble here to fight the foes the guardians fight now. Then, if we win, the destiny of this universe will be settled and new seeds sown. If we lose — it means chaos and eventual destruction."

"This is meaningless," argued Tallow, "you speak as if the world has united purpose. Surely every individual must discover his own destiny."

"Certainly," agreed the Guardian, smiling. "I agree. But he must never lose his links with his fellows — otherwise he is destroyed. Or else, worse for him, he joins the ranks of those we fight."

"You are demented, obviously!" Tallow sneered. "You are decaying here while you fight your imaginary battles. When a man has discovered his eventual destiny, the meaning of his life, then he will need no one. He will be gloriously alone!"

"I respect your views," smiled the Guardian, "but if you fulfil your quest, then you will realise what you have missed. Then it will be too late to go back and live according to what

126

you discover. It is always too late. You spend your lives chasing that which is within you and that which you can find in any other human being — but you will not look for it there — you must follow more glamorous paths — to waste your time in order to discover that you have wasted your time. I am glad that we are no longer like you — but I wish that it was lawful to help you. This, however, we may not do.

"You will be informed when you are to leave," he ended abruptly. "Now we must return to our fight." He got up, bowed and, followed by the silent eleven, passed, once more, through the door.

"Come on, Miranda," growled Tallow, taking her hand, "let's get out of this decadent madhouse!"

Miranda went with him reluctantly and once again they walked over the cool yellow lawn and entered the forest. They wandered on and then they were out of the dark wood, standing on the shores of a sea. It was a grey, heaving, timeless sea, a mysterious sea which stretched into infinity. There could be no other shores beyond this rolling plain of water. No other lands or rivers or dark, cool woods, no other men or women or ships. It was a sea which led to nowhere.

Over this timeless ocean hovered a brooding ochre sun which cast moody shadows of black and green across the water, so that the whole scene seemed enclosed in a vast cavern, for the sky above was gnarled and black with ancient clouds. And all the while the doom-carried crash of breakers, the lonely, fated monotony of the ever-rearing white-topped waves; the sound which portended neither death nor life nor war nor peace — simply existence, shifting in harmony.

They could go no further. Tallow clutched Miranda's hand and moved towards the ocean, but Miranda held back. He looked at her, his whole ugly face swathed in black shadow and scarlet — his eyes puzzled. She tugged at his hand and tried to move back into the forest; he hesitated, keeping her between himself and the tall trees.

"Come, love," He grinned his twisted grin. "Let us bathe in this dark sea! At last we may find what we want."

"No, Jephraim, let us return. I hate that ocean. I am sure it is what the guardians fight. Let us go back, Jephraim."

But he pulled her on, relentlessly, towards the shifting waters. She broke free and ran back to the edge of the forest, calling to him like a sea-bird. "Do not go, Jephraim! Do not perish!"

Tallow tried to continue his progress towards the ocean, but with Miranda gone, could not. He stood with one foot on the sand, as brown as dried blood, one foot on the yellow turf, undecided and afraid. "Would you have me perish alone?" he jeered.

"That is what you said you wanted!"

"No! I did not say that — I will achieve my destiny alone — and it is not in my fate wholly to perish."

"Then come back!"

The sea roared and tumbled, the sound of it increasing to a fury; daring Tallow to go on towards it, welcoming him with a wild temptation — offering him nothing but achievement — the achievement of death. He shivered and then he was running back towards the forest, feeling that the strange sea was pouring up the beach towards him. He looked back and saw that it had gone no further, that the breakers were less wild, the sea more calm. She gripped his hand with a frenzy of fear and hauled him towards her as if she had rescued him from a whirlpool. He clung to her and their bodies heaved in unison, locked and private. So they remained for a long time, while the sea called to Tallow and the wind was a cold caress on their flesh. But Tallow could no longer hear the sea and could only feel Miranda's warm body against him. In the bleak greyness of the alien shore, under a sun which gave no heat, their united bodies shone like a star in the night and once again Tallow knew the truth of companionship; a truth which he feared and hated while loving Miranda and all that she offered him. Even as they returned to the wood and lay down together by an orange tree-trunk on blue moss; even as he kissed her and spoke softly of his love, he was vaguely tormented and afraid of the consequences of his actions.

Hours later, Miranda said: "I wonder if the revolution was successful."

"I hope so," he whispered, "for if we are to go back, at least we have the chance of returning to friends."

"Shall we see if the guardians are ready to send us back to Rimsho?" she suggested.

"Yes," he said.

They began to retrace their way to the domed dwelling of the twelve fragile men. When they arrived, the man who had spoken to them previously awaited them.

"Walk on in that direction," he commanded, "and you will arrive at the place where you entered our land."

They went by him silently, through the clearing into the forest. They passed the silver river and saw golden birds again. Some time later they came to a place where the light seemed to shimmer like heat-haze and when they were beyond it they found themselves in the forest which lay to the west of Rimsho. Looking back they perceived that the unearthly trees had disappeared and ordinary woodland stretched behind them.

Something out of place swung like a pendulum back and forth across the path they had trodden on the previous day. Nearing it, they looked up and saw that it was a man hanging. A long-necked hawk-like man whose name had been Griff. He had an expression of astonishment on his white, dead face, a look which had been there even before men had come to hang him.

"Something's been happening, anyway," commented Tallow dryly. "Either Natcho's quashed the rebellion and is hanging those he thinks are traitors — or else this is one of Natcho's men and Zhist's followers have hanged him."

Miranda shivered. "Let's go on," she said, "and find a

129

gate."

They found a gate, jubilantly guarded by a member of the Free Fighters. He grinned at Tallow and leered at Miranda so that they were suddenly conscious that they were naked.

"Where have you been?" chuckled the soldier, who recognised Tallow.

"Fairyland," replied Tallow good-naturedly and went into the city leaving an astounded guard behind him.

At the first house they came to they knocked and borrowed a couple of blankets from the old woman who answered them.

The townsfolk were now really enjoying themselves, the fixed grins and glassy eyes had brightened and warmed. Zhist's soldiers were everywhere, taking advantage of the hero-worship lavished on them by the women of Rimsho. Tallow asked one of the soldiers where the Colonel might be found.

"Where else but in Natcho's old quarters?" laughed the man and turned once more to his bottle and his girl.

"Should have thought of that," said Tallow as he and Miranda, in blanketed dignity, strode through the streets towards ex-President Natcho's palace.

Chapter Fifteen

"I'M AFRAID CANNFER WAS KILLED IN THE FIGHTING," said Zhist with regret. Tallow felt only slightly elated that there was one complication less. Zhist went on: "As were many other brave men. He heard that you and Miranda were in trouble and was the first to reach the palace — he was shot down, of course. What happened to you two?"

"We were tortured and left for dead in the forest," Tallow answered. "We wandered in delirium for some time until we came to a stream. It has wonderful healing properties. Look, you can still see the marks of the lash. They are only scars now." He slipped off his blanket to show Zhist unasked-for proof of his ordeal.

"Miraculous!" exclaimed Zhist. "We must look for that river sometime. I suppose you've no idea where it was?"

"None," said Tallow truthfully. "I doubt if I could ever find it again."

"Pity," said Zhist. The food he had ordered earlier arrived

and the three of them sat around the desk at which Natcho had first interviewed Tallow and Miranda. They began to eat ravenously, for this was the first food they had had for some time.

"Hyriom's rumbling again," remarked Zhist, munching a roll. "They're growling about the Rights of Kings or something — say that our country's been overrun by a revolutionary rabble. This is the excuse they've been waiting for. They're going to invade us any day now — and we've got to be ready for them!"

"Good luck," said Tallow. He had just realised that Cannfer would have been more use alive. He could have taken Miranda off his hands. "I hope you succeed. In the morning I must be off. I've stayed for too long."

"You can't go, Tallow," Zhist said, "I'll need you here as my secretary."

"But I have delayed for nearly a week — if I do not hurry I shall miss the barge altogether."

"Forget about the barge, it can wait — follow me, instead. You'll be an honoured man in this city. And what about Miranda? Because of you she's been through hardship and finally torture. You can't desert her again?"

"He could," said Miranda, resignedly. "And probably he will."

"You understand, though, don't you Miranda?" said Tallow hopefully. He felt trapped.

"No," she said, "I don't fully understand. I would have thought that you'd have remained — now. But I suppose you'll do what you want to do in spite of me — in spite of Colonel Zhist — in spite of everyone who's attempted to be your friend and help you."

Tallow said doggedly: "Miranda — I've told you. I don't need help or friendship. Help of your kind serves to hinder me — friends delay me. I cannot afford the responsibilities which friendship — even help — affords. I am a man apart — a lonely man. I enjoy my loneliness."

"You're a strange bird, Tallow." Zhist chewed his food moodily. "A very strange bird. I can't make you out."

"I don't want to be made out!" replied Tallow angrily. "That's what I'm getting at."

"Can't make you out," repeated Zhist. "You appear to have no loyalties but those to yourself. Yet you didn't betray me under torture. From what you've told me of your journey down-river, you've attempted to help several people — and instead, have succeeded in ruining them in some way. You're a murderer — yet you don't act like a murderer. You have no motives, that I can see, for murder. You're in love with Miranda — and she with you. Yet you deserted her and are preparing to do the same again. What makes you tick, Tallow?"

"My mind," said Tallow, "that's what makes me tick — not my heart. Most men are ruled by their hearts — they use their minds to rationalise what they feel. With me it's mind first — emotions second, if at all. I never knew what emotion was until I first saw the golden barge going through the river. In that case it was emotion of some sort first — a *feeling*, you'd say — mind much later — if at all. I still haven't worked out what the barge offers me. But I'm sure it offers a great deal more than friendship, love, honour. These things will destroy me — make me one of the herd. I am not built for herd life. I can't exist among men — I haven't the mind, the physique, or the face. I don't enjoy the same things and I don't hate needlessly. I sometimes hate the things which interfere with me, but not for long. Miranda offers me comfort and peace of mind, satisfaction sexually, a lot of other things — but she cannot offer what the barge offers — whatever that is."

"Perhaps she can, only you don't see it," said Zhist.

"Don't argue with him," said Miranda. "Don't try — it gets you nowhere. I know."

"It's not my fault," Tallow said lamely. "It's not my fault, is it?"

"I'm sure if you remain among men and understand them,

133

let them understand you, you'll find what you're looking for," Zhist persisted. "You are the stuff of which idealists are made — the wrong kind. They follow their own personal star and attempt to make the world a better place — they wind up with the blood of millions on their hands — or their heads in nooses they've knotted themselves."

"I don't know what you mean."

"Listen," said Zhist. "These things which you — and a few others like you — want to find are right here. So many people go through life looking for something, trying to find it in money, in power, in sexual experience, even, occasionally, in painting, or music or writing. They don't know what they're looking for — yet something remote and unattainable seems to offer it. I'll tell you this — I offer it — Miranda offers it. That baby you found offered it. And you were too blind to know it! You're blinded by the glinting gold of the barge — seeking what you realise dimly as truth in something which doesn't involve responsibility of any kind. To find what you're looking for, Tallow, you must accept responsibility — accept friendship and love — even honour. They all involve responsibility. It is this process of *involvement* which teaches you the truth you struggle after!"

"Why should I become involved? Why? If it wasn't for you and Miranda, for people like you, I'd have reached the barge by now. Must I forever be plagued by people?"

"You are a man," said Zhist simply. "And a man has a soul — a life-force — call it what you like. There are millions of souls on this planet. Probably millions more in the universe. The very ground you tread has its own particular kind of soul — a sentience. We're all involved, Tallow. We can't escape the fact. We're all part of something huge. We're going forward Tallow. That's why I fought for the freedom of my people — it was my part in a far greater thing. That's why some men paint pictures — why some men go to war. You want something for yourself which all men should have. What will you do with your 'truth'

134

once you've found it? What will it tell you — it will tell you what I have told you — will you deny it then?"

"Impossible! What I want has no relation to what you've said. If anything I want the opposite."

"I can't convince you?"

"No."

Zhist sighed and stared at Miranda with resignation. "What do we do?" he said to her.

"Do? There's nothing we can do. I've tried to convince him — you have. Lots of other people have. We can only hope he gives up the chase and eventually comes back."

"The chase will become more desperate as it progresses," Zhist sighed. "He won't come back."

Tallow said: "Look — I'll stay for a few more days — then I'll have to go."

"Why are you relenting now — you said you were convinced that your quest was right?" Zhist got up and wriggled his shoulders, trying to instill vigour into his tired body.

"I'm not relenting. I shan't. But I'd like to rest for a short while and think. I'd like my boat checked over and plenty of rations aboard before I leave."

"I'll see to it tonight," promised Zhist. "Meanwhile — in the hope that you'll stay — you're my personal aide. You and Miranda can have Natcho's old rooms."

"Thanks," said Tallow. He felt hemmed in — first the position, now Miranda. He had lost part of his battle already. He was frustrated and, at this stage, could see no chance of surcease from the conflict he hated. *They're almost as bad as the people who imprisoned me 'for my own good', he thought. So many bloody do-gooders harming me and getting themselves harmed in the process.*

"I hope you'll leave me alone, for a while at least," he said.

"Certainly. I'll see you midday tomorrow if that's all right?"

Tallow nodded and left the hall. Miranda followed him, at

135

a distance. She smiled at Zhist as she went out.

Tallow and Miranda slept together but neither of them felt like love-making. Tallow was too worried about his dilemma and Miranda troubled about the future. They did not sleep well and Tallow rose early, pulled on the clothes Zhist had obtained for him and walked out into the bright dawn streets of the capital.

There was no one about. Most of the inhabitants had obviously caroused late into the night and had only recently gone to bed. Tallow's boots made a clatter on the cobbles and concrete of the city and the air was cool and clean to his lungs. The air, however, did not help him to clear his head of the thoughts which troubled him. He could not deny, though he wanted to, the fact that his conversations of the previous day had affected him. But, as far as he was concerned, there had been nothing constructive in the arguments of Miranda and of Zhist, all of which had followed a similar pattern and practically paraphrased one another. The arguments had served only to confuse and mystify him. He was as certain as ever that his path was the right one — he could not be deterred from it; but the inkling of other paths, equally as effective in their end, was causing him a great deal of consternation and more delays were imminent.

Torn bunting littered the deserted streets, flags were draped everywhere, over buildings, balconies, windows, lamp-posts. They flapped listlessly in the refreshing early-morning breeze. Rubbish of all kinds had collected in the gutters, where such existed; bottles of every kind, many smashed, the glittering glass scattered like diamonds over the streets, were in profusion. And then, Tallow saw the boy.

The child lay curled up amongst the rubbish, quite naturally. He did not look at all out of place; he was a piece of refuse himself with his ragged clothes and untidy hair. He slept, his face obscured by his crooked arm upon which his head rested. Without knowing just why, Tallow walked slowly over to the

136

child and pushed at the frail body with the toe of his boot. The child stirred and sprang awake, glaring up at Tallow with hideous yellow eyes streaked with red lines. The eyes, like the large unwholesome nose, were too big for the rest of his thin wrinkling face. His neck was scrawny and reptilian, the skin dry and scabby like a discarded snakeskin. He looked exactly like a tortoise; even his hunched awkward body resembling the domed shell, his huge nose dominating his sloping, almost non-existent chin, his big eyes having the hard quality of a rheumy reptile. When he spoke, he hissed hoarsely, thickly, the voice uncouth and jarring.

"What have I done?"

"Nothing that I know of," said Tallow. "Why aren't you at home?"

"Haven't got one any more."

Tallow nodded, silently, at a loss for anything to say in answer to this. He wondered why he had bothered to disturb the child and at the same time tried to guess his age. By his stature he was about nine or ten, the face could have been that of a new-born baby's; it could also have belonged to a grown man or a nonagenarian. There was no telling.

"Why are boxes always square?" enquired the boy suddenly.

"That's the easiest way to make them," Tallow answered.

"Then why don't they make them in different shapes? It would be better."

"Possibly," said Tallow gravely, wanting to go. The tortoise-boy turned his ugly profile towards the sun and got up; he stood looking at the sun in silence. Tallow was fascinated by him — he had never realised that children could be so ugly; usually children's faces were neutral, occasionally pleasant or beautiful. The boy's whole face and body were repellent; particularly his yellow eyes which now moved to regard Tallow. Tallow stared back, unable to do otherwise. They stood there in the centre of the street, looking into one another's eyes. Tallow experienced a peculiar sense of affinity with the unattractive child and said, at last, against his will: "We are outcasts, you and I."

The boy's voice was distant, it had a thick, dreamy quality: "Friends," he said. "Are we friends?"

"No. We are not friends. We could never be friends. Are dogs ever friends?"

"Dogs don't like me."

"Neither do I," said Tallow vaguely, trapped helplessly in the conversation. "You are repellent."

"Does that mean bad?"

"No."

"Nobody likes me at all. My aunt said I have the evil-eye. I can see as well as she can. My mother turned me out when my new father came. I do not want to be liked but it is hard."

"I know."

"What shall I do? I am lost here. I don't know what to do. What shall I do?"

"Stay here. You are better off in a place you're used to. Things may get better when you're older."

As they talked, their eyes continued to stare, locked as they contemplated one another warily as if they had met a perfect twin of themselves which they had never seen before. Yet there were differences. Tallow knew that this child was not sufficiently like himself to become a comrade, yet was too similar to be ignored. He had never suspected that there could be someone else so near to what he was. He wondered if there were others — other outcasts, misfits, aimless wanderers through existence. If so, why should they not be told of his barge — his aim?

"There is a barge sailing the river," Tallow informed the boy. "It is great and golden and is undisturbed by the tides which flow through the water, by the sun, or the wind. It moves with purpose. It is going somewhere and when it arrives, if you were there, it would help you. Would you follow it, given the chance?"

"No," answered the boy calmly, "why should I?"

"Because then you, also, would have purpose. The barge would help you, do you see?"

"I don't know what you mean. How can I be helped by some ship on the river? Will my aunt stop cursing me and my mother take me back if I see this ship? What good could it do for me?"

"You would know if I showed it to you. You would."

"You are a man — I am a boy. That is not the same. We are different."

"Only in age. One day I will show you the barge. Come with me when I leave and you will find what I have found."

"But what good will it do me? What has this ship done for you?"

"Nothing, yet," said Tallow sadly. "Nothing yet. But it will. Do you know others like yourself?"

"My sister," the boy said. "She is ugly. My mother lets her stay. My aunt gives her food. I know you — you are ugly."

"I don't mean others who look like you. Are there others who feel like you?"

"How do I feel?"

Tallow said carefully: "You feel alone. Unwanted. Unneeded. You feel that you need no one."

"Yes, that is how I feel. But I know of none like me. Should I?"

"No. I never did."

Tallow felt dislocated, out of his depth and his element. He was frantically searching for a word which would act as a key — as a link; something to make the boy realise that he was no longer alone. Tallow wondered if he did, indeed, need someone, whether the boy needed anyone, whether they were not both better off alone. The boy demanded nothing of him, was obviously beginning to feel restless. Desperately, Tallow brayed: "Come with me now. Come with me to the river."

"Why?" persisted the tortoise child. Tallow grasped him

139

and pinned his kicking limbs. He hoisted the boy in his arms and began to run. To his surprise, the boy did not shout, but he continued silently to kick and heave in Tallow's grasp. Tallow ran furiously and quickly down towards the river; he hoped that he would not be seen for this act might rank, however unwanted the boy was, as kidnapping.

Finally, he reached the river, unseen. His boat lay moored, half-full of the same kind of refuse which was spread through the streets. The whole river near the quay was full of bobbing bottles and wet, sluggish paper bunting. The corpse of a dog, swollen like a blown-up bladder, knocked against the side of his boat. He took a flying leap onto the deck and twisted the boy's arm so that he could not move without breaking it. Then he switched on the ignition and pulled open the throttle. The boat's engine began to chug into sluggish life, then roared with full volume and began to tug away, hampered by the mooring line. Tallow threw off the rope and guided the boat into the open river. He released the child.

"I can't swim," The boy rubbed his bruised arm and looked back at the city.

"You don't need to. The boat will not sink."

"Why are you doing this?"

"To help you," Tallow replied and stopped himself saying 'it's for your own good'.

Surprisingly, the child began to cry. "Take me back," he sobbed. "Take me back, please. You're frightening me. I don't want to go."

"Listen," Tallow hissed urgently. "Listen to me you brat. What I'm doing will give you a meaning to your wretched life. I'm taking you with me for your sake — not because I want you with me. Do you understand that?"

"No! No! You're taking me away from my home. I can't swim, the water frightens me. We'll drown!"

"It would be better for you to drown than to exist as you will do in Rimsho. You'll be friendless there — you will do

140

nothing of value. You will grow up, you will age — you will die. No one will know of your passing. This way, at least, I give you something to die for — a cause for living. Can't you realise this? Can't you? Ingrate!" Tallow calmed somewhat. "When you have seen the golden barge," he went on in a more consciously level tone, "when you have seen it you will know that what I am saying is true. You will want to follow it, also, as I am doing. We will learn what few of those fools back in the city will ever have an inkling of. Stay silent now, for I must make speed; I have lost too much time."

The boy subsided. His sobbing could still be heard above the throb of the engine as Tallow concentrated on the waters ahead.

Four days went by and Shoorom, the child, refused to eat more than the barest scraps required to keep him alive. He moaned in his sleep and was silent when awake. Tallow soon dismissed him from his thoughts and put all his energy into coaxing speed from his boat until, on the fourth day, the golden barge was jubilantly sighted. Tallow said nothing until the barge was much closer. As implacable as ever, it sailed on towards its mysterious destination. Then, when it lay ahead, dominating the entire river, he tapped the child on the shoulder. Shoorom started and turned his yellow eyes on Tallow.

"Yes?" he said, dispiritedly.

Tallow pointed at the barge and grinned. His face split into a wide gap. "There!" he exclaimed. "There's the barge, Shoorom. There it is!"

Shoorom looked unwillingly in the direction Tallow indicated. No new expression, as Tallow had expected, came into his eyes. He looked back, behind the boat and continued to stare at the water. Tallow was astounded at this anti-climax. "Well?" he said, impatiently. "What do you think of it?"

"Think of what?"

"The barge, of course, the golden barge! Wasn't I right?" Tallow could tell that the barge had had little impression and could not understand it; he had been certain that once Shoorom had seen the barge then he would admit that he, Tallow, had been right.

"What barge? I see only the river ahead and the river behind. I want to go home!"

"Look again," cried Tallow desperately. "Look again!" Dejectedly, the boy turned his head to stare, once more, ahead of him. He frowned and glared at the barge — and through it.

"What do you think of it?" Tallow said proudly, with the air of a man showing off a personal treasure.

"Please, Mr. Tallow, let me go home. I can't see anything at all. You're mad. Don't hurt me any more. I want to go back."

Tallow seized the boy's shoulders and roughly shook them. "You're blind!" he screamed. "Of course you can see it! Why are you tormenting me like this? You can see it — you must see it. I'm not mad — others have seen it. I'm not mad — others have told me. Stop tormenting me! Stop it! Stop it! Tell the truth, you brat — you wretch! Tell me you can see it!"

"Oh, I can't. I can't, Mr. Tallow. Let me go home. Please!"

Tears popped from Tallow's eyes and rolled along his nose. He switched off the motor and sank down on to the deck, his large head in his huge hands. "You're certain you can't see it?" he wept. "You're sure?"

"Yes — I'd see it if I could. I tried to see it, honestly. But I can't. Can we go back now?"

"Why?"

"I want to go home."

"I should throw you over the side. I thought you, if no one else, would see the barge. Am I really mad?"

"I don't know. Maybe only grown-ups can see the barge. Maybe children can't — just like children can see things grown-ups can't see. Don't throw me overboard!" The boy was shaking in terror.

"You want me to take you home?"

"Yes."

142

"Why won't you see the barge? This is your last chance for life. I am offering you the chance of great secrets — of truth. Why don't you try and see it?" Tallow was pleading now.

"Oh, I have tried, Mr. Tallow. I told you."

"You think children can't see it — you may be right. But then, I always thought that children knew more about these things than adults. I was wrong."

"Maybe children see things differently."

"You want to go home? All right. I'll take you home. Why, I don't know, for you've shattered a dream — I should hate you. But," he sighed, "I'll take you back."

Eight days after his sudden departure, Tallow reberthed in Rimsho. The quay was heavily guarded, but he was recognised and managed to get past the sentries with little difficulty. The boy scampered away from him and disappeared into a side-street. Tallow did not bother to stop him, or even bid him goodbye. He had long since lost interest in the boy and was glad to see him go. He wondered why he had taken the trouble to go all the way back to the city when he had been so near to the barge. He realised that he would have done such a thing only for the repellent child. Although his hopes had been shattered, he could not, after what he had done, desert Shoorom or drown him. The only thing he could have done was to take the boy back. Sullenly, disconsolately, Tallow wandered slowly towards the palace of the President.

When he got to the building, he reached his own apartments seeing no one but a few officials and soldiers. The place was full of rushing people and there was an air of urgency about the way they moved. Many carried papers or files — some had maps rolled under their arms. It was obvious that the expected attack by Hyriom was coming closer. In his apartments he found a note; it had had wine spilled on it and the stain was now dry. The note was addressed to him. Frowning, he opened it:

DEAR JEPHRAIM,
IF YOU DO RETURN — PLEASE STAY HERE UNTIL
I COME

Miranda.

Frowning still, Tallow folded the note and put it in his pocket. Curiosity made him remain in the apartment for two hours, then Miranda came in.

"Hello, Jephraim," she smiled, kissing him quickly as if she had seen him only a few hours earlier. "When did you get back?"

"Just now. What does your note mean?"

"Oh — that — I wrote it a week ago. Colonel Zhist wanted to see you. It was urgent — then. Where have you been?"

"For a trip on the river. I saw the barge again."

This plainly astonished Miranda: "Then why did you come back?"

"I'm not sure."

"Was it to see me? Was it? Or did Zhist convince you to stay, after all? Oh, Jephraim, I do hope so. Are you going to stay now? I'm very happy!" She was radiant, as she had been once or twice in the months before when they had been together. He couldn't answer her. He dare not, for he could only have answered her truthfully, and that truth would have hurt her in her present mood. She so obviously wanted to be happy. He would wait until she was in a different frame of mind. Meanwhile he might just as well occupy his time doing what he could to help Zhist. It would save him the trouble of having to explain things and also would stop him having to think too much. He took her by her shoulders, stretched on tip-toe, and kissed her on the mouth; she returned his kiss eagerly, in her old insatiable manner.

Later, he asked her, "Where's Zhist now?" She replied: "In the main hall. War is imminent and Zhist's test is near. The people look to him to save them from conquest by the Hyriomians. If he succeeds, then he is their leader, un-questioned.

144

If he fails, they will be a subject nation anyway, but their faith in Zhist as a leader will be broken — he will have no chance of rallying them. I hate to think what would happen."

Tallow heard this dispassionately.

Soon, a hideous plan began to form in his brain and although part of him attempted to quell the idea, another part argued that with Zhist gone, he would have no reason for remaining in the city — no one to shatter his complacency — no one to delay him. He hoped that Zhist might somehow die — and that the war would give him cover. He would escape in the confusion and Miranda would think him dead. So, effectively, he could dispense with all that was hindering him and could continue his quest in absolute peace. All this he thought as he led Miranda to the bed and began to unbutton her blouse. A decision had to be made — and now, he thought, he had made it.

Chapter Sixteen

"JEPHRAIM, I'M GOING TO HAVE A BABY!" Miranda smiled into Tallow's eyes. "It's yours."

"Wonderful!" exclaimed Tallow half-heartedly. More complications were combining to weigh him down and hamper his progress. "When is it due?"

"In four months."

Tallow was at a loss for anything appropriate to say. In the last few days he had been steadily growing back to become his old introverted self. All around him people moved and spoke, were grim, laughed; but he was detached from them, like a man watching a cinema film.

Tallow could not believe that he was part of it all and was growing impatient. He had still no methods with which to put his plans into operation and so he concentrated upon looking for the right circumstances. Zhist now only spoke to him and saw him when it was absolutely necessary — Zhist could no longer reach him and even Miranda was beginning to show signs of discomfort. She was studiously cheerful, trying to convince herself that everything was going the way she wanted it. But it was difficult with a blank-eyed, monosyllabic Tallow to deal with, a Tallow who made love automatically and whispered hollow endearments into her ears at night.

"Are you pleased?" she asked.

"Yes, of course," answered Tallow, wondering if he was ever going to escape from the traps he himself was making.

"Shall we have a boy or a girl?" she persisted, the gaiety in her voice becoming edged with strained uncertainty.

"Boy or girl. Fine."

"Boy?"

"A boy. Fine." Tallow knew that the war with Hyriom would not be put off much longer. A week or two at the most. He heard Miranda's voice again.

". . . name him . . . "

"Name him?"

"Yes, what shall we call the boy?"

"Call him Accursed!" said Tallow with dull rage. "Call him that if he's his father's son. Call him the Accursed and let him follow in his father's footsteps." He left the room, leaving Miranda wide-eyed behind him; tears beginning to form in the green depths.

She did not attempt to follow him. She remained standing in the room, her arms limp at her sides, hurt and troubled, her self-made dreams crumbling as she fought the madness she knew was inevitable. The madness which must come eventually to her and for which she must wait; she could no longer fight it. Her weapons were gone.

Tallow wandered the frenzied streets of Rimsho as the city prepared for war. He knew that a certain inn near the outskirts of the city was the headquarters of subversive politicos. This information had reached him in his capacity as Zhist's secretary and it had gone no further, for the men who plotted Zhist's downfall, whatever their reasons, would be useful in Tallow's scheme.

It was impossible now, simply to flee the city as he had
fled before, from other cities. He could not have done it. He
had to have a reason for leaving, something he had never had
before — other than the necessity of following the barge. He
was doing his best to manufacture a reason. He realised this
dimly, but dare not analyse why. To do that would result in
further indecision. Whatever force it was which drove Tallow, it
was at last beyond his control and he steadfastly followed a
decision which would result in doom and dark betrayal. He
could not help himself. He knew now that he had always realised
this. It was too late to change it. Too late to do anything but
tread the road he had chosen, for to step off it would mean
chuckling, screaming chaos and that he must fight if his barge
were to lead him to the knowledge that he desired. Toleration
was now no longer one of his traits. His own schemes had not
been tolerated — so he was learning that tolerance was an alien
thing to most men and their intolerance could only be fought
with that very weapon. Tallow let his decision to live and let
live sink away from him and he resolved, with grim anger, to
pay those who had driven him to the decision. To pay them
with a sample of their own philosophy. His thoughts confused,
his body sluggishly obeying the message of his chaotic brain, he
moved doggedly onwards towards the inn, uncertain what he
would do there but sure that any events would prove useful to
his dimly conceived plans, whatever happened.

The inn seemed an unlikely haven for political plotters. It
was a big place, with a hotel and restaurant attached, surrounded
by lawns of neat turf. Tallow remembered its name, The Black
Inn. It was a fashionable rendezvous for the rich of Rimsho.
The plotters probably reckoned that the customers of the Black
Inn were thought above suspicion.

As Tallow entered the main room of the Inn, he was hailed
by several groups of people who shouted good-naturedly and
beckoned him. He smiled back, politely, knowing that their

shouts were false and their beckonings those of men and women who thought that to have his ear was almost the same as having Zhist as a personal friend. It was difficult for the little man to realise that he was in Rimsho an important figure. He reckoned that it was not going to be easy to contact the plotters who would think him the last man capable of betraying the Colonel.

With a mental shrug, Tallow went over to join one of the groups.

Mr. Slorm, owner of the prosperous Black Inn, was puzzled. He had seen Tallow enter and had recognised him, though Zhist's secretary had never been to the inn before. Mr. Slorm was also worried, for he was a royalist. His business had been even better while there had been a monarch ruling the land. He was honest with himself and admitted his reasons. Upstairs, in one of the hotel rooms, other royalists plotted. And Tallow was downstairs. Had they been betrayed? Slorm tugged abstractedly at his long moustache which lay like drooping wings beneath his snout-like nose. His heavy eyebrows drew sharply together to form a single line over his deep-set eyes and he sucked thoughtfully on his few remaining teeth. Why was Tallow here?

Slorm was used to having many of his questions left unanswered. It was his nature to accept the situation as it came — although he would have preferred a monarchy he would never have troubled to alter the situation if he had not been approached by Largek and his friends. General Largek was one of the few military men who had served the exiled king and survived Natcho's regime. Now the General saw a chance to restore the monarchy. Slorm welcomed the chance and had risked letting the General use his hotel as his meeting-place. Beyond that, Slorm was not prepared to go. And Tallow's presence here might mean nothing — or it could mean the end of his, Slorm's prosperity.

Slorm decided to warn the General.

Tallow knew that Slorm was a royalist, and, when he saw the innkeeper run hastily up the stairs leading to the hotel apartments, he decided to follow. With a mumbled apology to his companions, he left the group and pursued the innkeeper silently. He saw him knock hastily on a door and enter. Tallow leapt after him on his long legs and reached the door as it closed. He bent and listened. He could hear nothing beyond a few hysterical murmurings from Slorm and the calmer grunt of the man to whom Slorm spoke.

Tallow delicately took hold of the door handle and risking his life and his hopes, danced into the room shutting the door behind him and leaning against it with an insane grin on his face.

"Gentlemen," smiled Tallow, bowing. "Your servant!"

Tallow had drunk three large glasses of wine and these influenced him. He was not drunk in the sense in which most men become drunk. Tallow was drunk in his own unique manner and now cared not a damn for anything, including himself. And this is not how most men become drunk, nor why. Tallow noted the looks of astonishment on the faces of the assembled plotters; he noted the look with delight and warmth, and he recognised General Largek.

"Good evening, General," he laughed. "Good evening, to you, sir. Good evening. Very pleased to see you here."

"What do you want, Mr. Tallow?" said Slorm nervously.

"Why are you here, sir?" demanded the General with a hastily assumed air of indignation. "Is there not a place in Rimsho where men can meet privately if they choose?"

"Of course there is, General. Of course there is a place. The Black Inn it is called and it's a den of royalists."

The General cursed and reached for his holstered revolver. But Tallow raised an arm. "Please — General — the dramatics are wasted, sir. Wasted. To shoot me would defeat your own aims."

"What do you mean, sir?"

150

"I mean that I'm willing to help you!"

"Why? You are Zhist's right-hand-man."

"Both right and left, my dear General," corrected Tallow. "He has no other. And so the right-hand knows rather well what the left-hand is doing. Luckily Zhist is unaware of the movements of either. You are safe — I shall not betray you. I have had the chance. Otherwise, why would I be here tonight?"

"Mr. Tallow, what's your game?"

"My game is your game, sir. Your game — up to a point. I've told you I'll help you. Only Zhist himself, could help you more than I!" Tallow was enjoying himself in his own drunken manner. He let the words babble out in a half-mocking flow.

"You are here to help us?" The General sounded disbelieving.

"Exactly, sir."

"Why — is this a trap? Some plan to get us out into the open? Why should you help us? We've heard of you, Mr. Tallow — we know you're cunning. You keep yourself to yourself and there are some who say you're the power behind Zhist."

This misapprehension amused Tallow and he laughed for several minutes, collapsing at last into a sitting position, with his back to the door. It was surprising, for this was the first time he'd heard the idea voiced. Still, it would not do to correct the General. If he thought that Tallow ruled Rimsho — so much the better for Tallow's plans.

"That's as may be." He tittered again, unable to control the reaction. "And perhaps you're right. The fact is that I'm willing to aid you. I don't care what you do. But Zhist must be got rid of. Exiled, preferably."

"Do it yourself. Why don't you engineer it yourself?"

"I need a good excuse. Couldn't manage it. Too many of the army people are on his side. I need you, gentlemen — and you need me."

"True.'

"Very true. I'll give you an excuse for rousing a mob against Zhist — you'll do the rest. Do you agree?"

151

"Conditionally," said the Colonel warily, unable to make Tallow's mood out. Seeing the look in the General's old eyes, Tallow began to laugh again. He chuckled uncontrollably and got up to plump himself down in a big armchair, from which the General had recently risen.

"What conditions?" he managed to gasp, as the chair engulfed him.

"How do we know we can trust you?"

"Well, you don't — you don't, General. And at this moment I don't know why you should. The thing is — I need your help — you need mine."

"That line of reasoning certainly appeals to me, Mr. Tallow. If you had said that you were a royalist, I doubt whether I should ever have believed you."

"I wouldn't have believed myself, General. Anyway, I never wanted to get involved with the revolution. Zhist blackmailed me into joining his men in the first place."

"Yes, I've heard that story. But why did you remain with him?"

Tallow decided that a lie he had prepared might appeal to General Largek. He said: "My — um — wife turned up unexpectedly. She fell in love with Zhist. I remained to attempt to take her with me. She would not go. If Zhist dies — or has to go away, I shall be able to convince her of her mistake in thinking she's in love with him."

"Ah," said the General knowingly. "Ah — jealously, eh, Mr. Tallow? Now I see . . . "

Tallow simulated a look of discomfort. "But we'll talk about that no more, General," he muttered. "Could you raise a mob?"

"I think so — but I dislike the idea."

"You have to use the methods of the enemy," said Tallow with conviction. "I'll make Zhist unpopular in certain quarters — you raise the mob. The rest will follow. Do you understand?"

"Perfectly."

152

"Fine," chuckled Tallow, laughing again at the seriousness of the General's demeanour. "Fine, my friends." He got up and bowed to the mystified civilians and army officers. Some of them bowed back. Tallow scampered from the room delightedly. "I shall keep in touch through Mr. Slorm," he called as he paced jauntily along the corridor and down the steps towards the main bar.

Blithely he ignored the chatter of welcome as he passed the groups on his way out. He waved a hand in uncertain salute and bounced towards the door.

Remembering the distance he had walked to get to the Black Inn, he decided to test his power. "Can anyone give me a lift?" he shouted suddenly.

A dozen voices chorused their willingness to aid him home. He selected the loudest and, with the man following him, pushed open the doors and went out into the night.

The man was big and beefy in the crested coat of a banker. He talked all the time and Tallow heard enough of his babble to interject a polite nod occasionally. The carriage was a four-seater affair, driven by a single coachman who commanded a pair of horses. The banker was obviously trying to get Tallow interested in a project which would see him and Tallow well set up for funds and the country rather the worse off. But Tallow, when he had made sense of the man's conversation, put on an expression of shocked horror, mumbled words like 'treason' and 'shot' which successfully drove the man into a frightened silence for a while. He had just begun to beg Tallow to keep the proposition dark when the carriage stopped outside the palace. Tallow disembarked, thanked the banker, treated him to a steely glare and hopped into the palace by way of a side-door.

Awakening the next morning with a dull headache and a return to his introverted, brooding mood, Tallow managed to get up without disturbing the pale-faced, tense Miranda and pull on his official uniform.

He had formed a plan as he slept, and he knew how he

153

could aid Largek and his friends and also start the events which should, if his plan worked, lead to his own freedom. It would have to be done very quickly.

Zhist, as was usual, had already risen and was in his office staring at maps, and worrying.

"Good morning," said Tallow with a worthy simulation of the previous night's cheerfulness. "How are you?"

Zhist answered with considerable surprise: "Good morning, Tallow. You're feeling better?"

"I am Colonel."

"That's a relief. I haven't been able to make you out these past days."

"Sorry, I've been worried."

"So I gathered. Where did you go last night, by the way?"

Hoping that Zhist did not suspect him Tallow answered truthfully. "To the Black Inn — I'd had news of plotters — royalists. I investigated the information and found the 'royalists' to be three or four harmless old men. They won't be any trouble — to arrest them would create unnecessary disruptions for us. Their friends might object and we would only succeed in feeding the propaganda fires of the monarchists."

"True," Zhist nodded.

"But I discovered something far graver," said Tallow slowly. "I discovered that some twenty of your officers are planning to desert to the enemy."

Zhist's eyes showed his surprise for a moment, then he said calmly, with a hard undercurrent to his voice: "How did you find this out?"

"From the royalists themselves. I pretended to be sympathetic to their cause and they gave me the names of the army officers they hope will aid them. Of course, they will be worse off if Hyriom wins the war — and they'll never get their king back. But the poor old fools don't realise this. I think the news calls for strong — and quick — measures."

"You're right! But — you're certain that the information

154

was correct?"

"Yes — I checked. You'll be surprised when you learn who some of the men are."

"Who are they?" said Zhist dully.

Tallow recited a list of names, being careful to name fifteen or so of the most untrustworthy men in the army and about five of Zhist's more dependable — and highly popular — officers. When he had finished, he said: "This is what's been worrying me for the past few days. I'd heard rumours — but that's all. What the royalists said last night confirmed the reports."

"Any ideas what we should do?" said Zhist brokenly. "I wouldn't have believed it of some of the men you mention."

"Nor I," agreed Tallow with veracity. "But the facts are there."

"We'd better round up those officers and hear their stories. See to it, will you, Tallow? With war so close we can't afford to risk allowing traitors to go free. It will make the men — and many of the citizens — restless, but we'll have to do it."

"I ll see to it," promised Tallow, and left Zhist to his maps.

He made his way to his own office and there wrote down the ranks and names of the men he had mentioned. Every one of them, as far as he knew, was wholly innocent of treason or anything else. An orderly entered the room in answer to a bell Tallow rang. Tallow put the sheet of paper into an envelope, sealed it and handed it to the orderly.

"Give this to Commander Partoc," he said. "Make sure he gets it and no one else." Commander Partoc was head of the Military Police.

"Yes sir," The orderly saluted and left.

Tallow sat back in his chair. He felt nothing — not even satisfaction. But part of his plan was already put into action. He could see no reason why the rest should not work. For a few hours he had to wait. Patiently, Tallow waited.

Barely two hours after he had sent the message to Commander Partoc, the orderly reappeared. He saluted and handed a sealed dispatch to Tallow. Tallow signed for the orderly to leave and opened the letter.

It stated that the twenty men had been arrested and that two had resisted. Bluntly the letter said that the men were restless and did not like the sudden swoop. It was signed by Partoc.

Tallow rang the bell and the orderly re-entered. "Ask Commander Partoc to come to my office," he said.

A quarter-of-an-hour later, Commander Partoc stood before Tallow. Tallow said: "Those officers you arrested. Colonel Zhist wants them shot."

"The men won't like it, sir."

"Have them shot, Commander. I don't like it either — but we all have to obey orders."

"Very well, sir." The Commander saluted smartly and, grim and grey of face, left the office.

An hour passed and the Commander returned. Twenty men had died by gunfire. Tallow nodded. "Good," he said. "Very efficient, Commander. I'll mention this to Colonel Zhist. It took courage to carry out that order."

"Thank you, sir."

Another hour went by and the orderly reported to Tallow. "Half the army's on the verge of mutiny, sir, over today's executions."

"I see," said Tallow, gravely writing. He sealed another envelope and handed it to the orderly. "Take this to Mr. Slorm at the Black Inn. Do you know it?"

"Yes, sir."

The orderly disappeared and Tallow sat back to wait. This time he waited four hours and he heard the mob in the streets outside the palace, just as Zhist sent for him.

Zhist was angry and worried. He strode about his huge office with huge strides. He turned sharply as Tallow entered and pointed a blunt figure at him. "Did you order those men shot?" he accused.

"Yes, Colonel, I did," said Tallow smugly He was certain now that Zhist was doomed. "I thought it would be best. It was clean and swift."

"Too bloody clean and swift — now half the city's up in arms against me. You've done more damage than those twenty men might have done between them!"

"I'm sorry, Colonel. I did what was best — for me."

"You did what was best. The country's finished now, because of that stupid order. Without faith in their leader they'll never rally to fight the enemy!" There was rage and horror in his voice. "All I've struggled for will be over in a few days — because of you!" He had not heard Tallow's last words, obviously.

"So what!" spat Tallow. "Does it matter?"

"You did this *deliberately*?" There was disbelief in Zhist's voice. "You *planned* this?"

"Yes."

"You knew that I'd be blamed for it?"

"Yes."

"Why, Tallow?" Now Zhist's tone was pleading; there were real tears in his eyes, whether of rage or of sorrow Tallow did not know. "Why did you betray *me*?"

"I owe you no loyalty — you said so yourself."

"But you did not owe me *this*!"

"I did — though you'll never realise why. I tried to reason with you. In a way you brought this upon yourself."

"What do you mean?"

"I can't explain again." Tallow had not realised that this interview would be so difficult. He found himself attempting to justify his actions. What was it about this fanatical little army officer which aroused unwanted emotions in him?

"But if you hated me enough to do this — what about all the innocent people who will suffer?"

"Damn the people. They don't matter. It doesn't matter if they die now or in a few years."

"It is not their lives I'm worried about. It's their freedom

157

— the freedom of their children. Don't you realise that? They have a right to freedom. They have a right to be individuals."

"Who gave them those rights?"

"I was going to give them the rights."

"Did they ask for them — did they ask you for them? Did they?"

"No — but they wanted them."

"Did they? They wanted food, air and sex — that's all they wanted. You decided — and men like you decided — that they wanted these amorphous rights. It was you who interfered — not I."

"Tallow — every man has a right to live as he wants to."

"Exactly. All you are doing is making him live another way. You are not letting him live as he wants to. A man lives as he *needs* to live."

"Your arguments are unimportant. How am I going to stop them doing something they'll regret?"

"Your actions are unimportant. They already regret deposing the king — Natcho — they'll regret deposing you when they have a conquerer sitting on Hyriom's throne!"

Zhist shook his head and turned his back on Tallow.

"I can't understand you, Tallow. I can't. I tried to help you."

"You've tried to help too many people, Colonel Zhist. Far too many people. Outside you'll hear their thanks."

The mob was roaring. Storming at the gates of the palace. A few sentries put up a half-hearted resistance but it was obvious that they were struggling between their duty and their sympathy.

"You said you wanted a tolerant regime," Tallow went on. "And your whole premise is based on intolerance. Intolerance of Natcho — intolerance of a political system That's how this started — you were intolerant of a fairly harmless system. You said it was harmless yourself — you said its fault was that it was 'outdated'. Toleration is fine — if everybody practises it, as I hoped to practise it. As I practised it once. Non-interference,

158

call it what you like. If you want your Harmonious Utopia — you can't be a politician. You must learn to be wholly tolerant and hope that it works — little by little, that way. You can't *enforce* tolerance, Colonel!"

"But I *loved* these people."

"I have never loved nor hated them, Colonel. I haven't the capacity for love or hate. Colonel — I have only just realised that I am more *of* these people than you are. I represent the 'mass', Colonel. I don't *want* to be helped. I just want to lead my life without interference, wherever possible. You decided to help me. Was it your love of me that made you make that decision?"

"No - oh, I don't know what it was. I'm not a bad man, Tallow. I don't deserve this betrayal."

"You're not a bad man, Zhist, I agree. But you deserve this — and more. I believe you or Miranda said that I regard people as 'Them' not 'Us'. I agreed with you, I think. Now I don't agree so much — I think I'm more of 'Us' than you or anyone else who accused me. I'm 'Us' because I don't think of it. I'm 'Us' because I don't attempt to help anyone. I'm an individual, certainly. Just as everyone who comprises the 'mass' is an individual until the politicians and the mystics and the do-gooders get to work on them. They're individuals because they don't stop and think 'I'm an individual'. Find a man, however, who admits to being one of the 'mass'. Find him, Colonel, and I might concede you have a small point — your point will be that you have an ability to mould a man's mind. I think I do hate you, Colonel, in my own way — because of what you represent — not because of what you are."

"You're wrong, too, Tallow. You know you're wrong." Zhist had collapsed over his desk. The mob was swarming in the square outside now, they had passed through the gates.

"I may be — but I don't think so, Colonel."

"Tallow — you forget your duties. I concede that you may have no rights — but you have duties — and those duties should

159

breed rights eventually. That's probably where they begin — as duties — but eventually they turn into rights. You have duties to your fellow human beings. You have responsibilities. By your very philosophy of non-interference you may harm countless people. If you try to help them, instead, you won't hurt them so much. I don't think I am as much a villain as you, Tallow."

"But where does it end, Colonel? Where is the line between helping the few and helping the many? Where do you leave off recognising your 'duties' and where do you start imposing new ones? Where does it end?"

Zhist sighed a deep sigh. He said: "Perhaps you're right. Maybe that sums up the whole problem of life and philosophy — 'Where does it end?' — I think we're both extremists, Tallow. We've gone in two directions — and both are the right ones — up to a point. Extremes are dangerous — and extremists are unhappy men — aren't we, Tallow? But is there a right direction which will not take us too far — or are there so many directions that we cannot choose? There are so many directions, Tallow."

"There are," agreed Tallow, "but I have found the true one." His voice faltered as he spoke and he fought off the nagging doubts which were invading his mind once more.

"But we can't stop this little turn of events now, Colonel," he said hurriedly. "Maybe I want to — maybe I don't — but I started the course — I made the turn. I must go with it to the end. You realise that?"

"I realise it. The same thing goes for me. If I hadn't forced you — and I suppose I did force you — to join me, I wouldn't be betrayed by you, now. We all start a wheel, Tallow. We start it turning and we must spin with it while we live. I am becoming a fatalist, my friend — as I think you are, too."

"Maybe" Tallow smiled viciously. "But I'm winning on this particular turn and I'll stay this way as long as I can." He regretted the pettiness of his words as he spoke them, but he followed them up with a pettier action. He was caught up in it now. He drew his revolver from his holster and pointed it at the

Colonel.

"You are my prisoner, Colonel."

Zhist shrugged. "So be it," he smiled painfully. "I'll not bother you. Will you kill me — or let me live?"

"Which do you prefer?"

"I think I'd rather live. I'd like time to think about our conversation — and the events which caused it. I'm not afraid of that," he finished defiantly.

"I'll try and see that you're exiled," promised Tallow, and meant it.

"Imprison me, if you like. I shan't mind."

"We'll see."

Three soldiers burst into the room. They carried rifles. They were mutineers. Tallow said quickly: "The Colonel is my prisoner — take him to the cells. Do not harm him."

The three men looked at each other.

"Do as I say," ordered Tallow, "I'm in command for the moment. You can lose nothing by arresting him "

"The people want his blood, Mr. Tallow. They want to lynch him!"

"What will they achieve by that? They've lynched so many people since the revolution."

"They want him, sir."

Tallow turned to look at Zhist. The Colonel shrugged once more. Tallow said: "Very well — let them have him." He did not meet Zhist's eyes again. He put his pistol back in its holster and the three soldiers grabbed Zhist and hustled him out of the room. The Colonel still had his lithe, animal vitality even as he walked away. He did not speak to Tallow but though he may have accepted the position fatalistically his body had not — it still had its energy, its power. Tallow felt a brief pang of sorrow and then the men disappeared and he closed the big doors behind them. He went to the window. The mob seethed — a grey mindless mass of protoplasm with only one thought now — Zhist's death. Largek and his men had done well — he had never thought them such good mob orators. It was Tallow's turn to sigh and he felt weary — he had none of Zhist's vitality.

Miranda came into the room. She was furious.

"What have you done?" she hissed. "What have you done now, Jephraim? Is this how you repay Zhist — with treachery? I thought you'd changed! And now you do this!" Her face was disgusting in its rage. Her voice was hysterical and her whole body tensed with a fury she could not express in words. She reached out and slapped his face. She kept on slapping it but he hardly felt it. He just stood looking out of the window until eventually she stopped. She followed his gaze. The mob had Zhist. They had ripped most of his clothing away so that he was incongrously clad in tattered underclothes and his boots. He was bleeding but still conscious. A rope went over a gargoyle which stuck out from the wall. A noose.

"No!" screamed Miranda. "No!" They can't do it!"

Tallow laughed — an unpleasant sound devoid of humour. "They're doing it," he said.

"Why did you let them?"

"I had no choice."

Now they had placed the noose over Zhist's neck. Men began to tug on the other end of the rope, hoisting the dangling figure up. The body twisted about for long seconds and then the boots clicked together three times in a military salute. Zhist said farewell and died. He hung there jerking, his face twisted, distorted by the constricting rope, his body stiff, soldierly to the last.

Miranda began to sob.

Tallow wished that he had managed to dispose of Miranda before his plans were put into operation. But it was too late now. He noticed that she was fatter; that her stomach appeared to have swollen. For the first time he fully realised that she was pregnant — with his child. 'My love child' he thought cynically, bitterly. 'What shall I do?' Suddenly he was sorry that he had done what he had — he regretted it. And then Miranda spoke again.

"I pity you, Jephraim Tallow," she sobbed. "I pity you — and I hate you."

"Don't hate me, sweetheart," Tallow said tenderly. "But at this moment I need your pity — and your help. I've never asked for help before — never. Now I need it."

She shrugged his hand away. "It's too late, Jephraim," she said. "Far too late. Only a day ago I might have helped you. But a day ago you refused my help. It's no good — you must take help when it's offered, or not expect it at all. I'm only human, Jephraim, unlike you."

"I'm human now, Miranda. Help me."

"Too late," she repeated and turned away.

Tallow felt as if he was swimming out of a deep pool and the pool was comprised of all the emotions he had feared. He seemed to reach the top and his head cleared and he reached for his pistol. Once more he was calm.

"Thank you for that, Miranda," he said gratefully. "You saved me with those words. But you have destroyed yourself." She turned, suddenly fearful.

"No, Jephraim!" she screamed, seeing the pistol, knowing his intent.

"No! You would not. You loved me — I loved you. No, Jephraim!"

He squeezed the trigger of the gun. It exploded several times before she collapsed. He did not look at her body. He dared not look. He was surrounded by corpses. Hemmed in by gigantic corpses which mocked him and accused him. Their accusations he could fight — but not their mockery.

Now he was uncertain what to do. He could flee — yet still he did not want to. Why? He could think of no logical reason The corpses alone were enough to make him go. Instead, his feet moving automatically, he went to the big windows which led to the balcony. He opened them.

Before he realised it, he was speaking to the people.

163

"My friends," he shouted. "Colonel Zhist is dead — the tyrant we served is destroyed. But our freedom is still at stake. Even now we are threatened by war — and if the enemy wins — we shall be a subject people. It will take centuries to throw off the yoke, once gained. We cannot fight the invaders — but let us give them nothing when they come! Blow up your factories and seek refuge in the woods and hills. Our only hope is to go far away and found new homes for our children. It is not entirely the fault of our leaders that we live this way. It is the fault of our cities — our society — our circumstances. Our greed is our downfall. Make a new start — or you will end your days in misery."

The wave of derisive laughter which wafted up to him was agony in Tallow's ears. He turned and fled. Now, his thoughts were at last only for his boat — and the golden barge.

Chapter Seventeen

NOW TALLOW PROGRESSES DOWN THE RIVER. His thoughts are chaotic, his actions confused. He feels like a cripple. He sobs sometimes and moans. At other times he laughs. He is frenzied but does not work with speed for his arms and legs are slow in obeying his mental impulses. He jumps about in his boat like a clowning fool. Nothing is harmonious. He is the antithesis of all the golden barge represents. Now the original yearning is gone — or is altered. It has been replaced by a frantic necessity. What the barge represents is no longer important. What it might offer is a question which no longer disturbs Tallow's pitiful mind. Now it is *habit,* sheer, unalterable habit which drives the wretch on. For something has rubbed off on our hero — he has ceased to be uninfluenced and this cessation contributes to his downfall. Plain, blunt, devious, blind, ridiculous Tallow does not even have his questionable faith any longer. He has lost it and strives ludicrously, in his madness, to find it again. He hopes that sight of the barge will bring a return to his earlier state of mind. But too much has happened and even in his weakness Tallow has become weaker. He has lost his dreams, cannot even remember what they felt like, he only knows that they were preferable to the mental situation in which he has found himself at last.

On he sails, and no longer bothers to ask *'Why?'*

Swirling echoes in his skull mock him. He still sees corpses, this little tragic figure. We can only laugh at him — and feel sympathy. Are we, also, among the mockers? We have followed his progress. Seriously? Facetiously? Cynically? With boredom? Troubled? Happily? How have we followed this idiot's progress? This blind man's caperings? This visionary's struggle? Poor Tallow. He has attempted too much, perhaps?

Tallow sails desperately on in chaotic frenzy. The wind fills the sails of the craft he has picked at random from the quayside. It is a very different ship to the little *Gorgon* in which he first set sail.

The wind in his face is balm to him, it soothes his poor, strained nerves. He realises that his teeth are tightly clenched together and deliberately, with the first coherent thought he has had since Miranda's death, he relaxes his muscles and parts his lips, breathing in the fresh, clean river air. His body aches and he has no idea how much time has passed since he resumed his disrupted journey. He cannot be bothered even to look upwards at the sun which glares down. All around him he sees only a misty haze of greenery and the shimmer of the silver water ahead of him.

His lungs are heavy in his body, his chest feels constricted and his head aches horribly. He mutters to himself sometimes and the words are meaningless mumblings; scrambled words without theme or construction. And tears glisten down his red face to fall upon his distorted nose and his wide mouth with lips set in a maniac's chilling grin.

Wretched and insane, Tallow keeps his long-fingered right hand upon the rudder-bar of his ship and guides it automatically,

166

sailing through the golden mornings and the bleak, black nights, passing towns, villages, cities, farms, and mansions and not seeing them, nor realising that they pass and, in his own way, Tallow sleeps and eventually the fever of fear leaves him and one morning he looks around and knows where he is and what he follows.

Rain is falling steadily, with angry vigour, and the skies are grey and sombre. The rain rivets into the river, stirring the water so that it swirls with increased energy about the boat.

And now Tallow falls forward. He collapses to the bottom of his craft and lies in dirty water, his breath coming in racking gasps, the water gurgling around his mouth, his starved, pinched features. He attempts to lift himself up out of the water. He succeeds at last in hoisting his weary body over a seat. Then he vomits liquid out of his stomach and consciousness leaves him.

Now a city lies ahead of Tallow's boat. It is a quiet city, a peaceful city of marble and mosaic, of green strips of turf and of stately people. But Tallow does not see the city, for he is still unconscious. His boat drifts on the river, at the mercy of a current which plays with it, whirling it around and rocking it. A tall man, in simple clothes which flow over his body, sees the boat and points it out, silently, to his companion, a woman of his own age with greying hair and a calm face. She looks at him for a moment and they speak. Then they turn quickly back and walk swiftly towards a large building on the quayside.

A few moments later men erupt from the building and run with long, easy strides down to where a boat is moored. It is a rowing boat, without sails or motor and it is slim with a high tapering prow. They climb into the boat and row in the direction of Tallow's craft which, by this time, is almost past the city

Deftly, they manoeuvre their own boat until they can touch Tallow's vessel. They attach lines to it and begin to tow it back to shore. They speak rarely and then only when it is necessary. They are a strange, silent people, apparently self-possessed and attuned to each other.

The shore is soon reached and the men gently take Tallow's gangling body in their arms and, with him cradled thus, place him upon a wheeled stretcher which awaits them. They push the stretcher towards a tall tower which stretches higher than the other buildings.

An hour later, on a bed, surrounded by puzzled people, Tallow wakes up and sees his rescuers.

He is unable to understand the circumstances and he is disorientated. The people surrounding him are silent and their eyes are sympathetic. One of them, the man who first saw Tallow, says:

"Do you wish us to help you?"

"No," replies Tallow, automatically.

"Then you may rest here until you feel like continuing. Or you may stay if you wish to."

"Where am I?"

"The City of Melibone," the man answers. He looks at his companions, but they cannot help him, they do not feel there is anything they can do.

"Where is that?"

"Fifty miles inland from the Sea."

"The Sea — it is so close. I had not realised. Tell me — " Tallow struggles up in his bed, his eyes intense, "Have you seen a barge pass? A golden barge?"

"Many times. Do you seek it?"

"Yes."

"You are not the first."

"So I believe."

The man is helpless. He cannot communicate with Tallow — cannot find the words which will warn him and which will not change his mind for him. At last, after an internal struggle with himself, he remains silent. By this time, Tallow's mind is wandering again and he, too, is attempting to tell the man something.

"I have seen sunsets and the stars. I have seen gay water

168

and dancing birds, pirouetting through the air." Although he talks on and on, Tallow does not communicate either. He wants to tell these people something, but he is unable to do so. No words come to him. "I have seen all these things in a year; never before."

The people around the bed are indistinct, their eyes stare, perturbed, at Tallow, at each other. They stare all the time and Tallow wants to tell them that which he cannot voice. He babbles on.

The people, also, are worried. Their code, an alien, almost inhuman code, forbids them to interfere in any man's destiny. But they are kindly people — they want to help him. They hope that Tallow will elect to stay with them. But they realise that this is unlikely.

"I am alone — yet surrounded — I am no individual. I am a blind man who has seen — a deaf man who has heard — but I am still dumb — as dumb as I have ever been. Why should this be? Is this the fate of every man — or is it my individual fate? Even the visions are not clear any more — the sounds are indistinct. Must I end my days in silence and darkness, when I desired — expected — light and words which were true? Too many questions. All down the river there have been too many. If only I had stayed on course. But am I to blame? No. Yes. I am both — and so are they. Oh, God, — where am I?"

Tallow's mind has been overwhelmed by thoughts filtering from the depths. Feelings — emotions — previously untapped, unexplored, unanalysed, surge up now and his brain cannot control them, for it has never known of their presence.

The people file out of the room, leaving Tallow alone, raving still.

"Why? Does a dog suffer this way? No — it is the suffering of a child. A child grown up too quickly — too suddenly to assimilate the data — too proud to heed the warnings of others. But were the others right — any of them? I was angry in that first town — they took away my individual rights — and now I

169

know there are no individual rights — only duties. Perhaps if I had stayed — no — no. But what of Miranda — could my yearnings have been satisfied — found fruition through my life with her — through the child which I gave her? Perhaps. That was better. And Zhist — could he have helped me? No. Miranda, Miranda — why did I kill her? Why? And Mesmers — perhaps — perhaps Mesmers? Mesmers and Miranda — they could have helped, if I had asked for the right things. But they only had certain things with which to help me. They did not offer all I required. Or did they? Uncertainty — it is horrible. Is it death I see ahead? Or is there still a chance in the barge? It is all I have now — I need it more than I ever needed it. Perhaps this is why I have been through all this? But must there be a reason? Too many questions — no answers. I am incapable of justifying my actions. Damn them! They have done this to me. They should have realised I was different. Or am I so different? Every thought brings a new question. I think there is still a chance if I can reach the barge in time. I must rest here, but only for a short while. Then I must continue. There is nothing *left* to do but follow the barge. Nothing."

Tallow's self-asked questions follow, repetitively. He desperately seeks an answer — one answer. But none comes. His sense of aloneness pervades his whole being; once again he is dependent entirely upon himself — but he is not so self-contained or self-reliant as he was. He has destroyed — and he has been destroyed. All that was strong in him — good or bad, whatever it was — all this confidence has gone now, crumbled out of him, leaving him only his weakness and a dream of regaining his lost strength.

Perhaps he has tried too hard — or not hard enough? He doesn't know. Indecision — the old indecision — has returned and it has been made more terrible because it is now abstract. He has nothing concrete to grasp.

For hours the questions still come and he seeks to shut up his mind, to forget the past and his hopes for the future. He is dreadfully frightened — his fear, perhaps, is the one tangible thing in his existence. But its very tangibility horrifies him and he would rather have it that nothing was tangible — nothing at all. In that way he might escape. More days pass.

He spends his time eating and sleeping. His waking hours spent in desperately attempting to assimilate his confused thoughts; his sleeping hours plagued by nightmares in which he sees the mocking, swinging, flowing corpses of those he has destroyed. Eventually he is physically fit again and he is taken to his boat and luck is wished upon him by the people of Melibone. They stand staring after him as he sets sail, dazedly, down the river.

Chapter Eighteen

I T WAS NOT LONG AFTER HE HAD LEFT MELIBONE
that Tallow glimpsed the golden barge again.

His sense of relief was something which thrilled through
his body and he speedily laid on sail in an attempt to catch up
with the vessel. But a bend in the river, then another, obscured
all sight of it. Tallow, for the first time in weeks, felt reassured
and was certain that he would sight it again.

Then, to his miserable disappointment, he rounded a bend
to discover that the river forked in two directions and the barge
was gone. Which way?

The long island which lay like a basking crocodile in the
centre of the river was in contrast to the leafy shrubbery which
thronged both banks. It had been settled. Without any apparent
plan, buildings were scattered upon it for as far as Tallow could
see. Very few trees grew there. The dwellings were hope to
Tallow — it was just conceivable that someone had seen the
barge pass and could tell him which direction it had taken. His

previous experiences had taught him to expect little; to expect
the possibility that no one had seen the barge; but it was his
only melancholy hope and he had to try to interrogate the
islanders, at least. He could think of no other course of action.

The island did not have a real quayside to which Tallow
could moor his boat, only jetties scattered haphazardly around
its shores. Selecting one which appeared to be of stronger
construction than the rest, Tallow tied up his craft and climbed
up the wooden ladder which led to the top of the jetty. A few
curious children stopped, gathered and stared at him, one or
two adults gave him a look as they passed, but none approached
him. There was no apparent order to the collection of buildings
and what streets there were appeared to be nothing more than
tracks winding tortuously among the houses.

Tallow tried to speak to the children first, but they just
laughed at him and ran away to disappear behind the single-
storey hovels which lay nearest the river-bank. The adults either
did not hear him, see him, or more likely, did not choose to
recognise his presence.

Eventually, one old man stopped reluctantly as Tallow
planted himself in front of him and bellowed a question in his
ear. "Have you seen a boat pass this way?"

The question seemed to have more effect on the old man
than it should have had. He looked startled and confused.

"May have done," he said at last, warily.

"What do you mean, 'may have done'? The boat is of
gleaming gold and follows a straight course, never varying,
putting in at no ports. Have you seen such a ship?"

"May have done — now I must go." The old man pushed
past Tallow and continued his progress, but Tallow walked
beside him, angrily repeating his questions.

"I must know — which direction did it take?"

"Don't remember — it was more than two years ago I saw
it — and thirty years before then. I've seen the bloody thing
twice and don't want to see it again."

"Which way did it go?"

"Never seen — and that's the truth. I followed it this far, thirty years ago — then I lost it. It frightens me, it does. Ask old Roothen — he'll tell you about that barge. I know it's a ghost ship."

Tallow did not attempt to stop the ancient as he tottered on his way. Old Roothen — what was the significance of that statement? he wondered.

He stumbled along, between the houses, with no idea where he was going. At dusk, he was almost a mile inland and had reached a place lighted by torches. It was a fairly large space devoid of buildings and in this space were gathered a number of people. Men, women and children sat on the ground or stood in groups, talking. The women were cooking over fires and the men had plates of food in their hands, or wooden beakers of drink. The gathering seemed to be some kind of celebration, for the people were laughing happily, enjoying themselves. Tallow walked up to one group.

He tapped a man on the shoulder. The man turned; he was white-haired and young with a thin, rat-like face. He said: "What do you want?"

Tallow asked him: "Have you — or any of your friends — seen a golden barge pass recently?"

The man belched in Tallow's face and turned back to his companions. He chuckled nastily. "This stranger wants to know about the fool's ship." The men laughed derisively, nervously, and looked at Tallow who stood there, uncertain of himself, hating them. One of them grinned crookedly. "Old Roothen will tell you about the ship, mate. He's been telling us what we already know for the last forty years and he'd like a new audience. We followed the bloody thing, same as him — but he says his case is different. I suppose you've come to tell us to go after it with you. If you have — you'd better find Roothen. We've got families to think of now. If he's not too drunk, you'll get a good story out of Roothen. He'll tell you."

174

"Where can I find him?"

"Follow your nose — you'll smell him."

"You don't know?"

"No — don't care, either. If your story's the same as his, I pity you. But don't tell it to us."

"I wouldn't," retorted Tallow, walking away.

He attempted to approach other groups, and received facetious replies. Soon, against his will, he was the centre of attraction and most of the hundred or so people in the gathering were staring at him.

"Who's that little man?"

"Some madman — trying to say the ship's real. We'd all still be following it if it was real. We were lucky enough to get out in time. Must be some river-madness that effects 'em. Why should this deranged idiot try and make us crazy too? You can't talk to him, though, not in a state like that — let's get him out of here!"

"What's he bothering us for?"

"That's what I'd like to know!"

"Coming here — spoiling our party. I knew it was going to be a bad day since I got up."

"Always was the trouble . . . "

"Think they can come here and . . . "

"Bothering us . . . "

"Why . . . ?"

"What . . . ?"

"Who . . . ?"

"How . . . ?"

Tallow's self-control broke: "Morons! You all went after the barge at some time. You didn't have the courage to continue or the will to go back against the current — so you're afraid when someone else comes along who has guts enough to take a risk. You think I'm mad — well I'll tell you something — I'd rather be mad than stagnating here like you!"

Someone tittered. A stone came hurtling out of the

175

blackness beyond the firelight. It caught Tallow a stinging blow on the wrist.

"Run away!"

"I'm going — " Tallow ran, concerned for his own safety. He had experience of crowds before, when he was a child among children. They had resented him then, and he had not known why. He still could not guess at any logical reason — but he had learned by his early experience. He could not stop them by shouting at them — he could only run.

He ran through the night, away from the torch-glare, and he pitied himself.

He lost his bearings and could not find the shore again so he sat down, panting, beside the first tree he came to, a big oak. No houses had been built near it. He sat with his back against the bole and wondered how he was going to find the mysterious old man the villagers had mentioned. Did Roothen really know something? Tallow wondered. He'd find out if he met the old man.

Dare he sleep — or should he go on, find his boat and make his own decision about which fork of the river he should take? As he pondered the problem, he heard a wheezing voice singing, seemingly from out of the sky. He looked upwards. There must be a man in the tree, he thought.

"Hello there, youngster. You're a sailor by the looks of you. Where you going?"

Tallow still could not see anyone. "Hello," he said cautiously, peering up into the branches. "I'm going down-river."

"Which fork are you taking?" This question was followed by a cracked, senile laugh.

"Not sure."

"Come up and join me!" There was a rustle of movement in the branches above and something fell down out of the air and struck Tallow on the right shoulder. He gasped and swore. He investigated the object and found it to be a rope-ladder leading upwards. With a shrug, he began climbing.

The ladder terminated about half-way up the tall tree and hung from a platform, crudely constructed, but strong and firm. Tallow pulled himself upwards, on to the platform and, through the darkness made out the pale face of an ancient, wrinkled man who grinned at him with a crooked mouth and eyes which hinted at strange madness.

"Who are you?" Tallow enquired.

"Roothen — old Roothen. I'm insane, you know — so the fools tell me. But I'm not insane — no more than you are."

"You're following the barge — or you know something about it?"

"What barge?" The question came cautiously, in a whisper like the rustle of dead leaves.

"The golden barge. Someone told me you'd seen it."

"Oh, I have — yes indeed. I've seen it. I followed it for three hundred long miles down-river." The old man was grizzling wretchedly and sickening Tallow. "I followed it, young fellow. Yes I did."

"Why did you stop here, then?"

"Why did you — why did the others?"

"I wasn't sure which fork to take."

"Neither was I, my friend, and neither were they."

"But — they say you've been here for thirty years. Is that true?"

"Thirty? Yes — it might have been thirty. It might have been more for all I know. Some have been here longer."

"Didn't you think of taking a chance — didn't you decide which fork?"

"Decide!" The cackle rose higher and died away like a sigh of wind. "Decide! I've been trying to decide for thirty years. Which fork — which fork — which fork? You know what it'll mean to take the wrong one? I'll miss the barge forever."

"Why? Couldn't you come back and try the other one?"

"Would there be time? Have any of those who went on ever come back?"

"There would have been if you hadn't waited thirty years. Why have you waited so long? The others may have found the barge."

"I've waited in the hope that I'd see the barge again and would know which way it went. I'm down by the bank most nights when I'm not too drunk. I drink a lot — I don't know why. I'll see her when she comes. She's elusive is that one — I've thought myself miles behind her and then I've been laying-to in port and seen her pass me by. I've missed her for days — weeks — and found her again as if she'd only been an hour ahead of me. What do you make of that? I've been delayed and held prisoner — but I've gone on — sometimes with blood on my hands. But I've always seen the barge — just ahead — just ahead, but never close enough to board and rip the secrets out of her. Why do you seek her, lad? She hasn't passed this way unless it was last night or a fortnight ago." Roothen ignored the second part of Tallow's question — he had no answer.

"It was last night that she passed, Roothen. I know because I followed her this far and lost her again."

"No!"

"Yes," said Tallow, almost delightedly. He felt nothing but contempt for the old man.

"Oh — you're lying to me. Torturing me. You're lying. Say you're lying, lad." The old man sobbed pitifully and Tallow heard him gulping at some liquid. "You are lying, aren't you?" He spoke anxiously.

"No," said Tallow, "I'm not lying."

The gulping noise again and a pitiful whining moan was all Tallow heard from Roothen.

"You deserve this," he said. "You deserve all of it — you don't deserve your dreams or your memories. You're a coward and a fool. You're as bad as the others — only you suffer different delusions."

"Don't say that!"

"It's true."

"No it isn't — I know it isn't. There's still time. I'm not that old."

"Are you young enough even to manoeuvre a boat?"

"Of course!"

"Are you!"

"Yes — yes! Of course I am. Take me with you, lad, and I'll show you. We'll risk it. We'll risk it, together. We're comrades, lad. We know something the others don't."

"We know nothing — we only know about something."

"Yes, but we'll know soon, won't we?" The old man moved forward, tottering towards Tallow. He clutched at Tallow's clothing and breathed foul liquor fumes into his face. "Take me with you, lad." He was pleading, whining, and Tallow was disgusted.

"Why? Do you deserve a chance? I'm strong enough to go on, my friend. Nothing will stop me from risking the rest of the river. I'll find the barge — and maybe I'll come back and tell you what it was. Shall I do that?"

The old man wasn't angered by Tallow's words. He continued to beg to be taken along, but Tallow shook the feeble hands off his coat.

"I've lost a lot, old Roothen — I've lost more than most men and I've lost my strength. I'm weak, Roothen, but not so weak that I can't continue, to find what I want."

"What do you want?"

"I'll know when I reach the barge. Where the barge leads me, I'll follow, until I'll know every secret that's ever worried me. I'll know the answer to every question which has ever come to plague me!" Even as he spoke, doubts were nagging in Tallow's mind, but he fought them down.

"Don't torture me, lad! Don't do that — take me along. I'll do my bit and we'll discover the knowledge together. I had a wife — I had a family — I had money. I've forsaken them all to follow the barge — and now I'm stuck here. You'd have pity on me — for I'm like you."

"No you're not."

"I am, lad. I am. There aren't many who've seen the barge — even fewer with the courage to follow it. We had the *courage.*"

"Curiosity," said Tallow. "It was curiosity to begin with, not courage. And our vision is suspect. Why should it be the best and only way? What secrets did we leave behind us? A man can discover his 'truths' by following many paths. I've found that. I've found that out too late — so I'm left with one path. A lonely path. I could have found what I wanted by remaining in most of the places I stayed at. I think this is why the barge leads men on — most of us, anyway. It leads us only a short distance, to show us something. But we don't realise that until it's too late to alter things. Finally, there's nothing to do but follow the barge on to the end and hope that it will lead you to an explanation of why you follow it. Why did you follow the barge? Why did I? Perhaps those who've settled here are right, after all."

"We followed the barge because we knew it had the truth. It was the only way."

Tallow looked up at the dark sky — at the small stars. He spoke distantly. "Were you as selfish as I was?"

"No — not selfish. I — I — just knew that there was a greater destiny offered to me if I followed it. I *knew* this, lad — I *knew* it!" The old man's feet scraped on the wooden planking.

"So I thought once, also."

"But it's true — don't let yourself think that it's not. It's true."

"Perhaps. It's all we have left." Tallow's disgust and his anger had calmed now, and he hardly realised the other man's presence. It was as if he were speaking to himself again, as he had done so frequently in the immediate past. "I must take the chance — or I'll end my days like you — fighting madness with a bottle."

"That's a cruel thing to say to an old man, lad."

"It's the truth."

"What of it?"

"Doesn't it matter that you're a drunken old dotard when you could have known the secret of life itself?"

"Yes — it matters; when I think of it."

"Then that truth should matter."

"I suppose it should. Go on, lad. Go on without me, I don't care. Probably you'll only get yourself killed. I'll have *life* anyway. How do we know that the barge is anything more than an illusion? Water plays funny tricks when the light's on it. It could be a sailor's madness — like these folk tell me. Couldn't it? A lot of people should know better than one."

"Do you believe that?" insisted Tallow, who was not sure what to believe.

"I don't know."

"So you rot here in your uncertainty. You might know whether you've wasted your life entirely, or not, if you followed the barge to the sea. You might find some kind of explanation."

"That's right — I might. So why not take me with you?"

"We've destroyed too much — you and I. I'm afraid we'd destroy one another."

"How? We'd help one another."

"Would we?"

"Of course. Look — we're both after the same thing. One of us could sail and the other sleep. That way we could keep going indefinitely."

"It's no good, Roothen. No good at all. I'm going. And don't try to stop me — I've killed too many people to worry overmuch about your death on my hands. Anyway — you're as good as dead!"

"You bastard!"

Tallow began to climb down the rope ladder. Palsied hands above him attempted to shake the ladder but the old man hadn't the strength to dislodge Tallow. He landed on the ground and set off again, in the hope of reaching at least one bank, which he could follow round and so find the place where he

181

had moored his boat.

The streets were unlit and the few people who were abroad did not even notice him. He felt slightly scared but not too worried. The villagers would, by this time, have found other diversions. He eventually came to a river bank, got his bearings and trudged along until he came to the jetty. Soon he was in his boat, once more, and attempting to decide which fork to take.

He decided at last to leave it to the current. He took the boat out and waited. Soon he was sailing down on the stream of water bearing towards the left-hand fork.

The water flowed swiftly and smoothly, almost with the same sureness of purpose as the golden barge. Tallow decided that if he was wrong and this was not the correct fork, then he would sail up-river again and take the other fork. But time, he felt, was beginning to run out at last. The old sense of urgency returned and he hoped desperately that he was on the right course.

Chapter Nineteen

THIS IS THE LAST STRETCH of the long, winding river. The river which runs from an unknown source down to an unknown sea. Imperturbable, it cannot be changed; only the banks change and the things on the banks. It is the life source of the cities and towns and villages which throng the banks — and it brings death. It brings hope and it destroys dreams. On it sail Tallow and a golden barge. We see it from above, see all its countless misty miles. We float over it and see only Tallow's boat; even we cannot see the barge at this moment.

Tallow struggles onwards and the water rushes ominously, gurgling and frothing; a sound which drowns all other sounds. But overlying this water-sound is a calm silence which speaks of great empty spaces and an eternity of peace. Tallow senses it — yet he is not insensitive of the state of the water, which predicts catastrophe. Tallow knows what the troubled waters signify. He knows but he cannot do anything. He is helpless — unable to fight that which he knows is inevitable. Faster and faster the

183

water rushes until it is a torrent dragging the unwilling boat with it.

At last Tallow's fears are realised and he sees ahead of him dark wet rocks, splashed by white spume, sharp, like the teeth of a yawning dragon. Rapids are ahead of Tallow; dangerous, deadly rapids — uncompromising in their stagnant power. Frenziedly, the little voyager grasps for the boat-hook which lies along the length of the ship. He lays it across the sides and grips the rudder-bar with hands that are white and which tremble with the tension he is experiencing.

Still the peaceful silence overlying the boiling, hurtling waters. Still the sense of solitude — of destiny.

Tallow acts. The first rocks rush past him and he is safe for the moment. There is the throbbing roar of the torrent in his ears. With marvellous dexterity, using his only innate skill, he steers the boat expertly through the rapids, his right hand on the rudder bar. With his left hand he deftly wields the pole, pushing the boat away from the closest rocks.

It is over. The rocks of the rapids are past him, and he sweats, trembles, moans softly. Now he knows he cannot turn back. His chance is gone. If he has not followed the correct course — then he is doomed. He cannot even return to the haphazard village where the river forks. He is completely alone at last, with no one to trouble him. He has what he desired.

The boat rides the water like a prancing horse, jubilantly dancing as if it has a will of its own. It rocks Tallow as it surges down towards the sea — swifter and swifter until at last Tallow cries out.

"Too late, my fine boat — too late to go back. Too late to dare — too late to destroy. It is finished now — for better or worse, it is finished. I am at the mercy of you — of the river — and of whatever fate awaits me at the river's end.

"Too late for my mother, Miranda and Mesmers. Too late for the power I could have had — the riches — the woman — the knowledge. Too late for peace of mind. I have it now — I have my lonely solitude!"

He looks down into the river which murkily mirrors his face. He sees, in horror, an older man — too old! He sees lines on the face which a greater passage of time should have brought. Pain in the eyes where, a year before, no pain was — only blank incomprehension.

Tallow is a man fighting madness with stone-wall methods. He is clinging to his last vestiges of pseudo-sanity — blocking any ideas or concepts which can shatter his terrible illusion. He is desperately trying to convince himself of something — but he can find no conviction which appeals to him. Every idea which comes to him, now, he rejects. He shouts to himself above the crash of water. He yells sentences and phrases — hurls them into the implacable silence.

"Free — I am free. Free at last to pursue the barge. I have gained much in my journey — now my yearnings shall be satisfied. I shall yearn no longer, for I have paid all prices! There is nothing left to pay. I have nothing else! I am free!"

The boat twists and turns, racing down the river towards the sea. Tallow laughs in a hideous imitation of joy. He throws away the boat-hook and releases his grip on the rudder. He stands up in the bobbing boat, and he spreads his arms wide, looking upwards and around him — calling, calling. Calling until the shout is all on one note — a chant which soon becomes meaningless — the words lost in his surging emotions.

And now he looks forward, suddenly. He cocks his head on one side in the old manner and he screws up his eyes to peer ahead. His eyes widen, slowly; they widen and his lips part. He stumbles towards the prow of the boat, but the river whirls it around. He moves jerkily, attempting to keep in sight that which he has seen. It is the barge, the golden barge — larger than at any time since he first saw it. He feels he can almost touch it. Like a miming clown he reaches out towards it, but the boat turns again. Desperately, he strives to keep it in sight and part of his mind regrets the impulse which made him throw away the boat-hook. He cries out — pleading — frantic.

"Save me — save me. You have made me what I am! Save me — have mercy! I am here."

The barge is sentient. Tallow knows that. It is alive and needs no crew. How can the barge help him? He realises that it has no arms to drag him aboard, no hands to reach out to rescue him. How can it help him? Tallow knows that he will never get aboard.

"Help me! You have led me to sorrow and madness — you have made me kill. I have even killed myself for you. I have made every sacrifice. I have made the sacrifice of blood, of misery and of terror. What other dark horrors would you have me experience before you will take me to you? Take me now — I have paid your price!"

It is obvious to Tallow that there has been no price needed. That his quest has been useless — unless he follows the barge to the end. He must continue to follow. He must. It is too early. There has been no price asked but tenacity of purpose. Still implacable, the barge courses on, unsullied by the water which derisively plays with Tallow's boat. His vessel is caught in a miniature whirlpool which spins it round and round while the barge continues on course, without variance of speed or direction.

Automatically, Tallow continues to call to it and he is reminded, against his will, of Miranda's shouts from the river, after he had thrown her overboard.

But a strange elation fills him and with a wrench on the rudder, he turns the ship out of the whirlpool's embrace and, battling the currents, sails swiftly in the golden barge's wake. It shimmers ahead of him, tantalisingly, seemingly omniscient. Is it God? Tallow asks himself as, with mounting jubilance, he hounds the barge. Is it God who taunts me so? He is still irrational — but with an irrationality born out of his impatient elation — not his previous morbid, rambling yearnings.

Faster and faster flows the current. Faster — down towards the sea. Now Tallow hears the surge of the surf on an unseen

186

shore — he sees, beyond the barge, a vast expanse of water, greater than any he has imagined. And his elation diminishes as doubt encompasses him. His fear of water — the old fear which he had of the river — his fear of depth — these fears grip him in a hideous embrace. Can he dare the ocean? But what lies at the river-mouth? Surely the barge will go no further? It is at the estuary that he will find his goal. He must.

As it nears the sea, the current becomes calmer, slower and the river widens. The barge keeps directly in the centre of the river. Continues onwards without pausing. Tallow shouts after it, the fear returning.

"No — don't betray me! Don't! Stay — come back. Not the sea. No, not the sea!" If the barge is aware of Tallow's presence, it makes no sign. On it goes, past the last land and out on to the ocean.

Tallow still follows — his sails bellying with the wind of the sea. His boat veers and scuds onwards, still in the wake of the glorious barge. As it sails over the ocean, which Tallow has not yet reached, a new iridescence radiates from it. It seems to swell to gigantic proportions; it is even larger than before. Tallow chokes in frustration and great tears well in his red-rimmed eyes. A huge salty drop careers along his nose and hangs there. More tears course down his face; they glisten in his stubbly beard. Onwards drives the golden barge — onwards towards the horizon. It is surrounded by massive depths of water on all sides. Mysterious ocean — more frightening than the dark sea which tempted Tallow on the day of Zhist's revolt. What is the ocean? Tallow wonders. Dare he cross it and follow the barge? But what will he find out there? Death? Or knowledge? Are they synonymous? Tallow does not know.

"I must decide, Now! I must decide. The sea is so great. My boat is tiny and I am even smaller. Dare I take the risk? Am I right? Is the barge what I believed it to be? Is it? If only I had a way of telling. If only it would show me some sign — then I would know — then I might follow it. But suppose I have been wrong? Suppose I have followed a dream of my own designing? No! Impossible! It cannot be true. It must not be true. I will not allow it to be true. The idea is false — for I know what the barge offers. I know it intuitively — deep in my ruined soul. Soul? It is my mind which is ruined. Mine was not great enough to take the strain. Or was it too small? Should I have taken the middle path? Succumbed to Miranda's temptation — to Mesmers — to Zhist? To the prison even? I know now that in any of these I might have found what I yearned for. But I demanded rights — and reasons — and tolerance. The human mind was never tolerant — or rarely so. Mine was not — though I thought it was, at one time. Intolerance breeds intolerance. There can be no unity — no harmony. We are all fragments, drifting after goals which half the time, perhaps all the time, do not exist. They are our hopes — our reassurances — some explanation for meaningless yearnings. There are only responsibilities — duties. If only we could talk to one another in words which mean the same things! Where is our end? Must we forever follow the golden barges? Must we forever drift down nameless rivers to nameless goals? To oceans which we dare not sail? Unable to share our boats, however hard we try? I wish I knew. Too many rivers — too many currents — too many tides. I am finished."

The boat slowly moves to a halt at the point where the river becomes the sea. It will need Tallow's guidance to sail it further. But Tallow makes no move.

Tallow sinks to his knees and his last defence against insanity breaks. He hears his own voice, clearly chanting a litany of madness: "Mother — gone. Murder! Miranda — gone! Blasphemy. Betrayal. Mesmers — gone. Destroyer!" His voice shouts on, listing his crimes as he sees them. He hears the sound of the voice but will not listen, knowing that to do so will engulf him in a final madness. A dreadful, black madness. He clasps his hands to his ears and sobs. The voice stops.

He grins triumphantly and stands up in the dangerously rocking boat, an old man, prematurely aged. A rotten husk.

But he twists his lips in a smile and his crafty head jerks to one side.

"I know the truth," he says. "I know it. And I don't need the barge. It was not courage I lacked to follow it. I need the barge no longer. It has taught me what I wanted to know. I have no longings, now — no yearnings. I am free of them, at last. Yes, Tallow triumphs, finally. And the barge has served its purpose."

A small, almost imperceptible voice within him keeps saying, *You are wrong. You are lying.* But he will not hear it — he rejects it. He will not listen. He dare not.

He stares in hopeless uncertainty as the barge reaches the horizon, still visible, still golden and gleaming, and disappears.